Ian had envied Mario for a long time, but finally had given up fighting his feelings and had requested a transfer to a different base so he wouldn't run into Ian and Gina together.

Not that he begrudged his friend's happiness; Ian just had a hard time controlling the ache in his heart every time he saw Gina's smile.

He'd done the unthinkable.

He'd fallen in love with a committed woman...his best friend's future wife.

So Ian had left. Run from her and his feelings, honor and integrity more important than his own selfish longings. It was the only way he'd be able to live with himself.

Now, she was calling him for help.

Someone had tried to kill her.

Like she believed someone had killed Mario.

Books by Lynette Eason

Love Inspired Suspense

Lethal Deception
River of Secrets
Holiday Illusion
A Silent Terror
A Silent Fury
A Silent Pursuit

LYNETTE EASON

grew up in Greenville, SC. Her home church, Northgate Baptist, had a tremendous influence on her during her early years. She credits Christian parents and dedicated Sunday School teachers for her acceptance of Christ at the tender age of eight. Even as a young girl, she knew she wanted her life to reflect the love of Jesus.

Lynette attended the University of South Carolina in Columbia, then moved to Spartanburg to attend Converse College, where she obtained her master's degree in education. During that time, she met the boy next door, Jack Eason, and married him. Jack is the Executive Director of the Sound of Light Ministries. Lynette and Jack have two precious children: Lauryn, eight years old, and Will, who is six. She and Jack are members of New Life Baptist Fellowship Church in Boiling Springs, SC, where Jack serves as the worship leader and Lynette teaches Sunday School to the four- and five-year-olds.

A SILENT PURSUIT
LYNETTE EASON

Steeple
Hill®

Published by Steeple Hill Books™

STEEPLE HILL BOOKS

Steeple Hill®

Recycling programs for this product may not exist in your area.

ISBN-13: 978-0-373-44362-8

A SILENT PURSUIT

www.SteepleHill.com

Printed in U.S.A.

I long to dwell in your tent forever
and take refuge in the shelter of your wings.
—*Psalms* 61:4

Dedicated to my daughter, Lauryn, who is growing up so fast. You're just beginning an exciting journey to discover the amazing plans God has for your life. Live each moment for Him. I'm so proud of you, sweetie!

ONE

"**S**top!" The voice shouted behind her, spurring speed to her already-flying feet. Stop?

Not if she wanted to live.

Rasping breaths escaped Gina Santino's throat as her bare feet pounded hard sand. She squinted into the inky darkness and her heart drummed in her ears, drowning out the sound of the waves crashing onto the beach.

She could almost imagine the breath of her pursuer on the nape of her neck. A hand reaching out to spin her around...

Goose bumps puckered her skin, but fear and adrenaline heated her body; sweat beaded her forehead.

The waves pulsed beside her as she stayed near the edge of the water, desperate to stay out of reach of the lights along the upper end of the sand.

Multicolored lights announcing the fast-approaching Christmas season were strung from the roof of the public beach–access restroom and briefly illuminated part of her path.

Long dark hair whipped into her eyes, blinding her as terror threatened to knock the strength from her legs. Her large antique locket bounced against her throat, matching the frantic beat of her pulse beneath it.

How had they found her? She'd been so careful. Yes,

she'd left her house in a rush, but she'd driven a crazy route that had her arriving at the beach house two hours later than the direct approach would have.

And they'd still found her. Her mind cramped at the possibilities as she flung a frantic look over her shoulder.

Was that a shadow? Were they still chasing her?

Of course they were.

Fear-induced adrenaline added wings to her fleeing bare feet.

Oh, Mario, I need you!

But Mario, her fiancé, was dead. Killed six months ago when a bomb exploded during a routine army training exercise.

Or so she'd been told. Who knew what the real story was? And now she was facing the holidays, Thanksgiving and Christmas, without him.

Of course, that was the least of her worries right now.

Driftwood crowded her path, and she jumped over another fallen piece of debris that had washed in at high tide.

Stumbling, she went to one knee, her momentum propelling her into the sand, rolling her over twice before she could push herself back up. Ignoring her screaming, sand-burned knee and oxygen-deprived lungs, she regained her balance, pumping her legs back up to full speed.

She couldn't keep running, not at this pace.

But she sure couldn't slow down.

He—they?—would kill her this time.

Please, God.

Her eyes darted, desperately seeking a hiding place. Shivers danced on her overheated skin as the freezing wind blew.

Up ahead, a light flickered. Someone walking toward her? She skidded to a halt, gasping, panting, sucking in much-needed oxygen; her knee throbbing a reminder that she needed to find a place to hide.

The light bobbed closer. Friend or foe? Had they surrounded her? Surely they couldn't have gotten in front of her. But then she wouldn't have guessed they would have been able to show up on her doorstep either.

What do I do, God? What do I do?

The safety of her little cottage lay approximately two miles behind her. Thank goodness she'd taken up running every morning for the last year. If not, she'd never have made it this far.

The light flickered, then disappeared.

A split-second decision had her making a sharp right to trudge through the softer sand. She didn't even have a cell phone. But the little diner just up the road would have a phone and she could call for help.

If she could get there.

A gunshot rang out, and Gina flinched when it hit the ground in front of her.

A warning shot.

That told her one thing. They wanted her alive.

And that scared her more than the thought that they might want her dead. She double-timed her struggle through the sand, praying that whoever was chasing her was having the same problems. Finally, her feet hit asphalt.

Another gunshot. She cringed, expecting at any moment to feel the pain of a bullet entering her body. She pressed on.

She needed a phone.

She needed help.

Where was Ian?

Ian Masterson pressed his foot to the gas pedal. He'd promised Gina he'd be there at 9:00 p.m. It was now 11:45 p.m.

and the darkness pressed in on his windshield like dirt on top of a coffin. She'd called him yesterday and asked him to meet her at the beach house. He didn't have to ask for directions. Gina's cousin, Antonio Santino; her late fiancé, Mario Anthony; and he, Ian Masterson, had been the Three Musketeers.

Best friends and fellow U.S. Army Rangers—no three men had a tighter friendship. Until Ian moved away. Then Mario had died and Antonio had flown off to Iraq on a mission. Ian was home for the moment and would be until Gina's troubles were resolved.

But he'd been held up on the way to meet her. He'd had to request emergency personal leave to get out of a last-minute assignment in Pakistan. Fortunately, a buddy with another unit had volunteered to go in his place.

Ian owed him big time.

Only now he was almost three hours later than he'd said he'd be, and Gina wasn't answering her phone.

He didn't like the thoughts crowding his mind.

Punching her speed dial button one more time, he offered up a prayer on her behalf.

Her voice mail clicked on again. He hung up and clenched his teeth. *What were you working on, Mario, that's put Gina in danger?*

She hadn't told him much when she'd called yesterday morning asking him to meet her. Just that some men had tried to kill her when she'd walked in on them tearing her house apart in Spartanburg, South Carolina. Now, she'd fled to the coast and trouble had followed her.

His gut clenched as he pictured her face. Dark hair, with upturned black eyes that hinted at Asian ancestry some-where back in the Italian family line. He clearly remembered those eyes, which hid her innermost thoughts but could flash with compassion or laughter at the drop of a hat. The next-to-the-last time he'd seen her had been about eight months ago, when he'd stopped in to see his old commanding officer and had overheard her in the hallway. She'd been moaning about losing weight so she could fit into the wedding dress she wanted. She hadn't known he was there. He'd left as quietly as he'd arrived.

The last time he'd seen her had been at Mario's funeral. She'd lost the weight.

Ian's fingers clenched the steering wheel. His molars ground together as he remembered Gina's devastation at the funeral. He'd gone to her and offered her a hug, but her stares were like daggers cutting through him, the accusation clear in her liquid-chocolate eyes.

She might as well have shouted the words, "If you'd been here, he wouldn't have died."

But she didn't, just hunched her shoulders against her grief and walked away.

And caused Ian a fresh bout of crippling pain.

Ian had envied Mario for a long time but finally had given up fighting his feelings and had requested a transfer to a different base so he wouldn't run into the two of them together. Not that he begrudged his friend's happiness; Ian just had a hard time controlling the ache in his heart every time he saw Gina's smile. The way she tilted her head to the left when she really listened to what you were saying. Or the way she pulled her hair back into a long ponytail that revealed her slender neck. He'd watched her pulse beat there one time and had to leave the restaurant they were in because of his overwhelming feelings for her.

He'd done the unthinkable.

He'd fallen in love with a committed woman.

His best friend's future wife.

So, Ian had left. Run from it and his feelings, honor and integrity more important than his own selfish desires. It was the only way he'd been able to live with himself.

Now she was calling him for help.

Someone had tried to kill her.

Like she believed someone had killed Mario.

His cell rang and he punched the button. "Hello?"

"Ian?" Short breaths rang over the line, as if she was out of breath. Relief flooded him at the sound of her voice, his protective instinct kicking into high gear at the thought of her in danger. "It's me. Gina."

"I know who you are. Are you all right?" he demanded.

"No," a hitch in her voice clamped hard on his heart. "Someone's still after me. I'm at the diner on 17." She didn't have to explain which one; he'd been there enough times with Mario. "Can you pick me up there? How far away are you?"

"Stay put," he said. "I'm about three minutes from you."

"Oh, thank you," she breathed. He could almost taste the fear flowing from her as she whispered, "Hurry."

His foot pressed the pedal harder. He'd told her he was three minutes away. He'd do his best to make it in ninety seconds.

TWO

Gina hung up the pay phone and, ignoring the occasional strange look from the diner patrons, scurried to the window. Her breath still came in pants although she'd recovered from her run. It was the terror still quaking through her that stole the air from her lungs. She'd been so careful. How had they found her?

Probably her cell phone. They'd obviously tracked her with no problem and had, no doubt, laughed all the way up the highway.

Mario, what were you up to? What did you hide? And where did you hide it? Who were you hiding it from? I don't even know if you were one of the good guys now.

Tears clogged her throat at the betraying thought. But she didn't let them fall. She never would have thought he'd do something to put her in danger, and yet by dying, he'd apparently done just that. It had taken six months, but obviously he'd led the trail straight to her.

Headlights flashed in the parking lot.

Bad guys or Ian?

She looked at the clock on the wall. About a minute and a half had passed. The lights flashed once more. Then again.

Ian.

She bolted out the door into the drizzle, which had started the minute she'd entered the restaurant. Her bare feet slapped the wooden porch, then the steps. The door opened from the inside.

Throwing herself into the passenger seat, she slammed the door just as a bullet pierced the windshield to bury itself in the backseat.

Ian hissed, put a hand on her head and shoved her down in the seat. "Hold on!"

"I'm so sorry I had to drag you into this," she squealed.

"We'll get to that later." He threw the gearshift lever into Reverse and screeched from the parking lot. Another bullet hit the back windshield and shattered it.

Glass flew.

Ian drove.

Gina prayed.

It seemed like hours, but in reality, according to the dash clock, only seven minutes had passed since the last bullet.

"I think I lost them." He grunted and turned left.

She pushed herself into a sitting position, brushing stray bits of glass from her legs and hair, careful not to cut herself. Turning to the man beside her, she gasped, "You have perfect timing."

"Actually, I was running late due to an unforeseen circumstance with my commander, but I'm here now and you're in more trouble than you let on."

"When I called you, I didn't know how bad they wanted me."

"Why call me? Why not the cops?"

"Because they'll just turn it over to the army."

"And that's a bad thing?"

"It is if there's a traitor on the base."

That shut him up. Then he asked, "Who?"

"I don't know. All I know is that Mario died during a training exercise. At least that's what I was told. Who *really* knows what happened?" Sarcasm dripped. "But if that's the case, then someone set him up."

"How do you figure?"

She remained silent for moment.

"Gina?"

"I don't have any proof. Just a gut feeling. And I know you'll think that's crazy, but someone has tried to kill me twice, so I'm leaning on trusting my gut at this point in time."

This time he paused as he glanced in the rearview mirror, then the side. "Sometimes your gut's the only thing worth trusting."

Tears flooded her eyes. "Thank you," she whispered. "I don't know what Mario had that these people want. I mean, I'm just a real estate agent from a small town in South Carolina who happened to fall in love with a guy who had a lot of secrets—ones he didn't bother sharing with me. Or couldn't share. Who knows? I don't know anything except that they think I have whatever it is they're after. Which means I need to figure out what it is and find it before they find me. And I think I need your help to do that." The words spilled from her in one breath. She finally paused and drew in some air.

"I would say you're on the right track." He gave her a gentle smile, and for the first time since her mad dash into the car, she noticed his rugged good looks. She'd always thought him a handsome man, had actually been attracted to him, but had been so committed to Mario, she'd ignored those feelings.

Tonight they returned with a rush.

Wow.

Immediately, she felt guilty. As if she'd just betrayed Mario in some way. It must be the terror-induced adrenaline spiking her senses into hyperawareness. She looked away.

Forcing her thoughts to focus on the important thing—like getting away from a killer—she said, "I had to slip out of a back window at the beach house. I've got nothing on me. I don't know whether to go back to the house and try to get my stuff or have my parents wire me some money. I'm sure they're already worried enough. I don't want to add putting them in any kind of danger."

He placed a hand over hers. "I've got you covered. Let's find a safe place to hole up and hash out what just happened. Then we can worry about other necessities."

Ian found a little out-of-the-way hotel room and asked for two rooms. Gina stood beside him, shivering, her bare feet probably frozen. He had one person in mind to call whom he trusted, no questions asked. Jason Sutton. A man whose skills as a Ranger had saved Ian's hide on more than one occasion. A onetime fellow Ranger in the same unit Ian and Mario had served in and a good friend to them both, Jase would come through for him—he hoped.

Finally, they made it to the rooms. Gina entered hers and Ian followed her in. He chose the desk chair, while Gina sat at the table, hands clasped in front of her. Wild dark curls had found freedom from the pink scrunchy that now encircled the lower portion of a ponytail gone bad. She didn't seem to notice.

"First," he said as he set his bag in the second chair, "I've called my sister, Carly. She's a U.S. marshal who's going to come stay with you tonight to protect you while I focus on looking for the guys who just tried to kill us. The faster I'm able to get on this, the faster we'll figure it out. Now, the marshals aren't officially on this case, you understand? She's just doing this because I asked and should be here in a few minutes. But for now tell me everything you can, Gina. Who's after you?"

She lifted burdened shoulders. "I don't know, Ian. All I know is that they want something and haven't found it, yet."

"Which means they'll keep coming back until they do."

She grimaced, rose and walked to the sink. The sound of running water reached his ears, as did the crinkle of plastic covering being torn from a glass. She filled the tumbler and took a long drink.

Sighing, she placed the glass by the sink and paced back to the table. She looked him in the eye. "You knew Mario. Probably better than anyone. He trusted you enough to order me to contact you should something happen to him—and weird things start happening to me. Someone tried to kill me— not once, but twice." She held up two fingers for emphasis. "I'd say that qualifies as weird enough. You're here. Now what?"

Nothing like being put on the spot.

Ian stood and paced from one end of the room to the other. Then he turned and said, "Tell me about the first time some-one tried to kill you."

She shuddered and his heart pinched at the distress on her pretty face. A face strained and drawn with the stress that had become her life. "Not my favorite topic of conversation."

"Come on. I need to hear the details." He gestured toward the other chair and said, "Have a seat."

Gina rubbed her eyes, gathered her strength and started. "I had just gotten home from work, having closed on a great house. Everything had gone smoothly, and I was feeling better than I had in months. When I got to my house, I didn't notice anything wrong. My neighbor pulled into his drive about the same time I did, and I remember waving to him. He waved back and walked to get his mail. I walked up to the door and it was locked. I had to use my key like always." She swallowed, closing her eyes as she visualized each detail of that day. "I opened the door, stepped inside and someone grabbed me from behind. He put something over my head." Her breathing became shallow pants at the remembered terror. She had been certain she was going to be raped and killed.

Ian's hand reached over and grasped hers, holding it in an almost painful grip. She flexed her fingers and he let go. "Sorry."

Clasping her hands together between her knees, she hunched her shoulders, took a deep breath, then let it out slowly. Leaning back and staring at the ceiling, she said, "I managed a pretty good scream before they stuffed a rag in my mouth. If they were going to kill me, I was going to make them work for it. I kicked one, got my hand free and managed to get the rag out of my mouth. I remember screaming again."

This time his hand squeezed her shoulder, and she could feel the tension emanating from him in waves. "I'm sorry to make you recount this, but I've got to hear it."

"I know. It's all right. It's just…" She shook her head and he encouraged her with the compassion in his eyes. "Then the one who had me from behind whispered in my ear, 'Scream again and I'll slit your throat. Now, where is it?' He pulled the rag from my mouth and I asked him what he was looking for. He said, 'Mario stole something from my boss and he wants it back.'"

"What did his voice sound like?" Ian interrupted. "Did he have an accent?"

Gina scrunched her nose as she tried to remember the voice and not the fear. "Maybe a slight one. He whispered so I can't…no, he didn't have any kind of distinguishable accent." Then her head shot up to look him in the eye. "But the other guy did. In fact, I think he spoke a couple of Spanish words."

Ian raised a brow. "Spanish, huh?"

She shrugged. "Maybe."

"Then what happened?"

"I screamed that I didn't know what he was talking about, that Mario never told me about anything he stole. Then my neighbor was banging on my door, yelling my name and asking if I needed help. That's when we could hear the sirens coming down the street. The man holding me shoved me to the floor, and then they all ran out the back. At about that time my neighbor kicked the door in and said he'd called the police when he'd heard me screaming and through the window could see me struggling with someone."

Ian ran a hand over his face. "Thank God your neighbor was home."

"I know. He was early that day and so was I. I usually go to the gym around that time, but in spite of feeling so great about the sale, I had a headache and wanted to go home and lie down for a bit."

"So you changed your routine that day."

"Just a little, yes."

"They probably weren't expecting you to show up."

"You mean I surprised them?"

"Yeah. If they wanted to get in your house to do a search, most likely they'd been watching you for a while to get a good idea of your routine."

"And I picked that day to alter it." She closed her eyes and shook her head.

"Unfortunately." Ian stood and paced to the other end of the room, then back. "And that started it. They may have been trying to find whatever it was that Mario had without involving you, but once you walked in on them…"

Gina nodded and frowned. "So that's why it took them six months to come after me?"

"Maybe. And yet why let on that they were looking for something specific? They could have just acted like it was a robbery and left without saying anything."

Silence descended, surrounding them as they lost themselves in their thoughts.

"They're out of options," Gina stated quietly.

Ian focused in on her. "What do you mean?"

"They've probably been looking for whatever it is that Mario took since the day he died. Six months later they still haven't found it. I'm the only link left."

An almost imperceptible nod came from Ian. "You could be right."

"So what do we do now?"

"Well, we keep searching and keep avoiding whoever's after you until we find it."

"I have a feeling that's going to be easier said than done."

Ian shrugged. "Guess we're going to find out. I called a buddy of mine, Jason Sutton. He's going to bring us some supplies. Stuff my sister can't get her hands on or I'd have her bring it."

Recognition lit her dark eyes. "I know Jase." Then a frown formed between her brows. "But I don't know that Mario trusted him anymore. I know they had some kind of conflict going on shortly before Mario died. Unfortunately, I don't think Mario trusted any of the guys from his unit." Her gaze softened as she stared at him, and a flicker of confusion passed over her pretty features. "Just you. He trusted you. Why?"

Discomfort made him turn from her straightforward look. He couldn't share that information with her—yet. Under the guise of checking the street, he walked to the window, stepped to the side and pulled back the curtain a mere centimeter.

Nothing.

He turned back to her. She still waited for his answer.

"Mario knew I'd never do anything to hurt him. Ever. I guess he realized that in time and—" he paused and shrugged "—sent you to me. Also because..." He stopped, the rest of his answer hovering on his lips.

A knock at the door sounded.

Pulling his gun, he checked the peephole, then returned the weapon to its holster. "That's Carly." Relief at the reprieve filled him, and he opened the door. A young woman in her early thirties, with the same blue eyes as her brother, stepped into the room.

Ian shut the door and gave her a hug. "Thanks for doing this."

Carly grinned up at him. "Always loved the night shift." She turned her gaze to Gina, studying her. "Hi."

"Hi."

Ian stepped to the door. "I'll let you guys get acquainted, but I'd make it short if I were you." He looked at Gina. "Get some sleep, it's already almost 2:00 in the morning. We'll talk about this tomorrow."

Gina blinked at Ian's sudden departure.

Well. Then she narrowed her eyes. He was getting out

while he could, avoiding any more questions he didn't want to answer. She let him go, moved to the bed and sank onto it.

Carly settled herself into a chair, facing the door yet away from the window. "So, you've got someone after you, huh?"

"To say the least."

Compassion softened the features she shared with Ian.

"Why don't you get some rest? No one will bother you tonight."

Fatigue hit Gina like a truck, and instead of getting up and taking the shower she'd planned on, she fell back to stare at the ceiling. "Thanks, I appreciate that." Then she sat back up. "I think I'm too exhausted to sleep."

Silence reigned for a moment; then a sympathetic Carly asked, "How did you and Mario meet?"

Gina smiled at the memory. "He wanted to buy a house."

"Ian told me you're a Realtor."

"Yep. Mario wanted to buy a house in North Carolina. I was working with a firm there, and he got put through to me. We met and the rest was history as they say."

"Did he ever buy the house?"

Gina chuckled. "Not in North Carolina. He eventually bought the one near Myrtle Beach. The whole thing in North Carolina was an undercover deal. The president was going to be at the Charlotte Coliseum. There had been reports of a terrorist attack there, and Mario was assigned the case. My real estate office was right across the street from the Coliseum. It made for a good cover."

"And he called you after the mission was finished?"

"Yeah." Her eyes grew heavy and she gave in to the desire for sleep, murmuring, "I think I might be able to get a little rest, if that's okay."

"Go right ahead—that's why I'm here. I brought a book

to read." With that she opened a thick novel and conversation ceased.

While Gina's body demanded rest, her mind wouldn't shut off. What had Mario been thinking? What had he been involved in that would cause someone to come after her?

Racking her brain produced nothing but a headache, so she turned her thoughts to Ian—what was it about him that caused Mario to trust the man? Why, of all the people Mario knew, did he practically order her to contact the one person who—in his eyes—had betrayed the unit by leaving?

Okay, if she was honest with herself, she'd have to admit *betrayed* might be too strong a word. *Deserted? Bailed on? Abandoned?*

Whatever the word, he'd left the unit and, as a result, disharmony had ensued. The team recovered, of course, but it was never the same. And while Mario had not shared the details of everything, she knew he blamed Ian for the fallout. He'd been quite vocal about that because the guys had never really liked Robbie Stillman, Ian's replacement.

She rolled to her stomach. *Lord, I need you. Please help me figure out what I've gotten myself in the middle of. And take away this weird attraction I feel for a man who has as many secrets as the one I lost.*

She must have slept, because the next thing she knew, she awakened with a start, heart pounding, at the click of the door closing.

Who was there?

Where was Carly?

THREE

Ian paced in the tiny area between the two beds and the small bathroom, glancing at his watch again. Carly had just knocked on the door to let him know Gina was still asleep and she had to get going to report in to her day job. He regretted her lack of rest, but it couldn't be helped.

As for himself, he'd slept a little, dozing until Jase called to say he was on his way. Night had passed without incident. He could only hope the day would go as smoothly. Something told him not to hold his breath.

He pushed the curtain aside just enough to see out.

Where was Jase?

Jason Sutton and Ian had served together under Commander Mac Gold. Jase was a dedicated man and in love with patriotism; Ian couldn't remember the guy ever making a mistake on his watch.

Three short raps swiveled his attention to the door. Crossing the room in three long strides, he knuckled back two short knocks.

One tap answered.

Ian opened the door.

Jase, tall and dark as midnight, slipped into the room, silent as mist. "I made it as fast I could."

"Thanks, buddy."

"Haven't heard from you in a long time." Ian picked up on a coolness in the man's voice that hadn't been there before he'd left the unit.

"I know. I'm sorry." He left it at that.

Jase grunted. "Whatever."

A rap on the door brought both of the men's attention to it. Ian walked over, peeped out and then opened the door, pulling Gina inside. "Gina, what are doing? You don't need to be out in the open like that."

Spying Jase, she drew up short, her eyes taking on a wary look. "I heard the door shut and it woke me up. I thought…" She shuddered. "Anyway, Carly left me a note saying she had to leave and that you would be over shortly."

"Yeah, you should have waited on me."

"I'm sorry. I'm just ready to get back to work on this." She looked away and over at Jase. "Hi."

Ian saw what she didn't offer. She was scared to be alone. He didn't blame her. Laying a hand on her shoulder, he said, "You said you knew Jase. We were all in the same unit once upon a time. Jase transferred out right before Mario was killed to be closer to his extended family. I asked him to bring me some things. I also told him what was going on with you. Unfortunately, he doesn't know much more than we do at this point."

"But I told you…!" Panic glistened in her dark eyes even though she'd known he was going to make the call.

"I know, Gina, but Jason's okay. He's not part of that unit anymore. He was gone before Mario died."

She wilted back onto the bed. "I didn't mean any offense by my reaction, Jase. It's nice to see you again."

His lips quirked as he nodded his bald head in Gina's direction. "Don't worry about it. It's nice to see some things don't change," he teased softly. Gina never had been very good at hiding her feelings, and Jase had gotten to know her pretty well. She flushed and looked away only to appreciate it when Jase said, "Mario was a good guy. I've got some contacts I can ask to put out some feelers about him, if you like."

"Thanks." She bit her lip, then seemed to make up her mind. "Do you know anything he might have been involved in? Anything that he might have had that someone would be after?"

Jase shrugged. "No. There's no telling. We go under-cover all the time. Sometimes as a whole unit, sometimes as a partial. And we don't always get filled in on what the others are doing unless there's a need. There's just no way to know. I saw him several times over a period of a few weeks before he died and thought he was acting strange. But when I asked him about it, he shrugged it off and never let on he was having a problem."

"Strange how?"

Jase shook his head. "Nothing I can really put my finger on. Withdrawn, moody, quick to anger—and late to a lot of meetings. Just—stuff that was unlike Mario."

She nodded, and Ian wanted to put his arms around her; then he caught the sheen of tears in her eyes and decided he might need to offer her his shoulder to cry on.

Instead of doing either one, he held a hand out to Jason. The man looked at it for a moment, then slowly reached out to shake it. Ian couldn't read Jase's expression but thought he saw something soften in the other man's eyes. Jase offered, "Call me if you need anything else. I'll keep after the other guys in the unit to talk to me and see if any of them know what Mario was doing right before he died."

"I'd appreciate it."

Jase's eyes flicked to Gina, then back to Ian. "Take care of her."

Then he was gone like smoke on a breeze.

"He's a little different than I remember," Gina murmured.

Ian turned to Gina, who sat on the bed. "What do you mean? Different how?"

She shrugged. "Of course I never saw him in the field, just when we would all get together and have cookouts or eat out or whatever. But I seem to remember that he was always the life of the party, the prankster."

"Yeah. I remember that. But you're right. In the field, he's like a different person, rarely cracking a smile unless the situation calls for it. Total professional."

"So, what did he bring?" She gestured to the backpack.

Ian looked inside. "A high-security laptop, night-vision goggles, an assortment of weapons, a GPS and—" he reached in and pulled out a device "—an encrypted cell phone."

"We're going to need all of that?"

"I sure hope not."

"Huh."

She seemed to lose interest in the topic. He lowered himself into the chair across from her. "Are you okay?"

She blinked. "No, but that doesn't matter. I want to go back to the beach house and search it. I got interrupted before I had a chance to do anything. I…didn't exactly start searching the minute I got there."

"Was that the first time you'd been there since Mario died?"

Lips tight, she nodded. "Yes. I just walked on the beach for a long time, remembering the good times, the fun we'd had. By the time I got back to the house, I was hungry. I fixed a sandwich and went back into Mario's little home office. I'd just opened the desk drawer to start searching when I heard the front door squeak. It only took a moment to realize it wasn't you." She closed her eyes at the memory, and Ian clenched a fist, wanting to pound those responsible for her fear.

Opening her eyes, she said, "So, I climbed out the window and took off down the beach. I must have made some kind of noise—I think I knocked something over—and they were after me pretty quick. Luckily, it was dark. I think that's the only thing that slowed them down. That and the fact that I knew the beach and where to cut through to get to the diner."

Regret filled him. "I'm sorry I was so late. I should have been there to…"

"It's all right." She stood. "But now, I'm going back to the house to see what I missed—and what damage those goons no doubt did to it. Mario willed it to me, you know. I was his beneficiary for his estate. Everything."

"He didn't have any other family?"

"Just a mother out there somewhere. He hadn't seen or talked to her in years. He finally decided she was dead."

"That's a shame."

"I know."

Ian rubbed his chin thoughtfully. "You know, they may have found what they wanted back at the house. If they found it, you may be safe and they won't have any reason to come after you again."

She looked up at him, then said slowly, "Or they found it, think I know about it and will want to make sure I don't live to tell anyone about it."

Ian blew out a breath. He'd thought about that but hadn't wanted to mention it.

But Gina had already analyzed this from every possible angle and come up with some of her own answers.

He stood and pulled a pair of shoes from the bag Jase had brought. Handing them to her, he said, "They look a little big, but I guess they're better than nothing. Come on—let's go see what we can find out."

Going back to the beach house was fine, but Ian wasn't going back blind. Grabbing his phone, he punched in Jase's number. "Hey, you offered to help, so I'm going to take you up on it. I need you to do one more thing for me."

They drove in silence, Gina keeping her eyes on the rearview mirror and the road behind them, although she couldn't see much in the early morning darkness. "Do you think this is a good idea?"

"Probably not, but I think it's our only option right now. As much as Mario loved that house, it's probably where he'd stash something important."

"You knew him so well. He loved you like a brother. How could you…" She trailed off, unable to finish the sentence that had his fingers curling around the steering wheel and turning his knuckles white.

"Gina…"

"Why'd you leave, Ian? I mean, I know people transfer to other units for reasons like Jase's, but what was your reason? No one understood why you requested the transfer. And Robbie Stillman." She grimaced. "No one liked him. He was always such a jerk. If you just could have given them a reason…" she blurted out. There. She'd finally asked the question that had been burning in her mind for the past two years. The question not even Mario had been able to answer.

Silence greeted her. Just when she thought he wasn't going to answer, he sighed. "It was a really personal issue I was struggling with, Gina. Maybe one day I'll share it with you, all right?"

She stared at him, catching the inner agony of his blue eyes before he turned them back to the road. "All right. I guess I have to accept that...for now."

"Thanks." And he said no more. The silence in the car draped as heavy as the flag over Mario's coffin. Gina shifted in her seat, uncomfortable, worried about what they'd find back at the beach house, yet she couldn't deny the relief she felt at having Ian at her side.

"Why don't you lean that seat back and shut your eyes for a while?"

"I wouldn't be able to sleep. I can't believe I actually slept at all last night." It hadn't been a deep, restful sleep, but she'd definitely dozed.

"You were tired and you've had a huge shock, mentally and physically. Sometimes our bodies have to override our brains."

"I guess."

"I asked Jase to go ahead of us and check out the house."

Her nerves stood on end. "First the hotel, now this. I told you Mario didn't trust his unit."

"I know, but like I said, Jase isn't part of that unit anymore, and the only way we're going to figure out what Mario was involved in is to talk to the guys who were the last ones to see him alive."

Biting her lip, Gina looked away, wondering how to say what she was thinking.

"What?" his tone sharpened as he caught the look on her face. "What is it?"

"Nothing."

"You don't lie well, Gina. What is it?"

"I just…" She blew out a sigh.

"I think I know what you're trying to say."

"You do?"

He squeezed the steering wheel again. "Yeah. You don't think any of the guys in the unit will talk to me about Mario because they consider me something akin to a traitor, right?"

Gina blinked against the resurgence of tears and whispered, "Something like that. Although Jase seemed okay with you."

Another moment of silence passed as he concentrated on his driving. Then he said, "I never betrayed anyone by leaving, Gina. Contrary to popular belief, my leaving probably saved the unit."

"How?"

His jaw tightened. "It's not important. What's important is that we figure out what Mario was involved in and what led someone to come after you six months after his death. If the guys won't talk to me, maybe they'll eventually open up and talk to Jase. I'm going to have to trust him until he proves otherwise."

"So, what are we going to do?"

He shot her a look. "Bait the trap."

Ian made several phone calls on the way back to the beach house; however, he made sure no one knew where they were going. Using the encrypted phone Jase had supplied, Ian didn't worry about anyone tracing his calls.

At first, Gina listened in; then Ian watched her lids grow heavier and heavier, the restless night taking its toll. Finally, they shut for good and he could see her even breathing indicating sleep had won.

He glanced at the clock: 5:30 in the morning on what would be a cold but bright, sunny day. Right now the temperature hovered in the low thirties. Gina's questions still pounded at him. When he'd said his leaving probably saved the unit, he hadn't been exaggerating. Mario knew how Ian felt about Gina simply because Mario had a reputation for playing the women. And Ian called him on it.

After a mission several years ago, they'd all been out celebrating, and Mario had started responding to a woman's flirtatious advances. Ian walked up and asked him, "Is Gina so easy to forget?"

Mario took a swing, which Ian dodged, then hauled his friend out of the restaurant. Out on the sidewalk, Mario narrowed his eyes. "You're in love with her, aren't you?"

Stunned, Ian hadn't responded at first. Mario had taunted him. "I see the way you look at her. How your eyes follow her every move. Admit it."

In silence and without responding, Ian had clenched his jaw and his fist—and walked away. For good. His transfer request went through without a problem, and within two weeks he was part of another unit.

Forcing his thoughts from the past, he dialed Jase's number once more. His buddy answered on the first ring. "Where are you?"

"About ten minutes out. What's it look like?" Ian kept his voice low, not wanting to disturb Gina.

"Clear for now. Because of Gina's worries, I came to check it out myself instead of finding someone from the unit. The house is a mess, though. They're looking for something."

"Has anyone noticed and reported it to the police yet?"

"Not that I can tell. It's pretty isolated out here. Mario liked it that way."

Ian hesitated. "Are you willing to keep helping me out a little more on this, Jase?"

Silence on the line.

"Jase?"

"Whatever it takes to keep Gina safe. She didn't deserve to lose Mario the way she did. She's still one of our own." A pause, then, "So, yeah. I'll do whatever I can to help her."

"What about me? Do you think I betrayed the unit by leaving?"

More silence. "You could have told us why you were leaving. Maybe we could have worked something out."

"Mario knew."

Jase grunted. "He didn't share."

Ian didn't think he had. "Yeah."

"Right. See you in a few."

Ian put his own phone away, thinking. He trusted Jase, but it was quite possible Mario hadn't. Or was it that he hadn't trusted the unit as a whole? Or maybe he had suspicions about one particular person, but no proof, so he had to isolate himself from everyone until he figured it out?

That was probably it. He knew someone was bad but didn't know which someone. What information had he come across to make him suspicious of one of his team members? What had he seen or been told?

And now Mario was dead. Blown away on a routine training exercise. Not that accidents didn't happen on occasion, but…

Hands down, Ian was willing to bet Mario had trusted the wrong person. None of his paranoia about whom he could trust had paid off. He'd died anyway. Possibly killed by one of his own.

The question was—who?

The possibilities were endless.

And Jase had been a member of that unit.

Now Ian second-guessed himself. Had he made a mistake in trusting Jase? Surely not. The man had saved his life on more than one occasion. Had saved Mario's, too. Although he could be a prankster upon occasion, he was definitely a dedicated professional when the situation called for it.

And then there was no more time to dwell on it. The turnoff for the beach house came into view, and Ian swung onto the little side road.

The driveway needed repaving. Gina jerked awake just as Ian decided to cut a path around to the back of the house and park right at the back door. Jase had assured him the area was clear, but it never hurt to be prepared to leave fast.

"We're here."

She blinked up at him, sleep fading and reality returning—along with remembered fear. His heart thudded as he resisted the urge to grab her up in his arms right that very minute and promise nothing would ever hurt her again.

Not a promise he could make. Waves crashing against the shore pounded his ears. That special Christmastime ocean smell filled his nose, and he breathed deeply while his eyes probed the dark shadows. Uneasiness trembled through him.

Too many places to hide.

Too many possible dangers could be lurking nearby.

Keeping an eye on the surrounding area, he walked around to the other side of the vehicle and opened Gina's door for her.

From the corner of his eye he registered movement at the left side of the house.

He shoved Gina back against the seat, ignoring her startled gasp of protest. He slammed the door and grabbed for his gun in one smooth movement.

FOUR

Heart pounding, Gina froze. What should she do? What had Ian seen? From her scrunched position, which had her halfway over in the driver's seat, she could see the top of Ian's head through the window. He'd pushed her back into the car and left himself open. Had her attackers returned to wait for her?

Scooting fully into the driver's seat, she cranked the car and hit the headlights, illuminating the area in front of her. If they had to leave fast, she wanted Ian to be able to jump into the car immediately. She could see a figure on the fringes of the light. He waved a hand and looked like he said something.

Ian holstered his gun as the man came toward him.

Now she recognized him.

Jase.

Relief sucked the breath from her. She pushed the door open, gave a shiver as cold wind buffeted the car and climbed out in time to hear Ian say, "Man, you should give a guy some warning before coming out of the shadows like that. I could've shot you."

Jase barked a short laugh. "Not you."

"I thought you were gone, and when I saw someone moving around out here…"

The man shrugged. "Thought I'd make sure there wasn't anything that was going to jump out and scare you when you got here."

"Yeah, right."

A ghost of a smile crossed Jase's face. "From what I can tell, it's clean. I went inside and looked around a bit, but didn't want to disturb too much in case you wanted a forensics team to come out here and see what they could find. The rest of the time I've been watching. There's been no movement, nothing. There's no one here."

"Great. Thanks. What else?"

"I made some phone calls."

"To whom?" Gina blurted as she rounded the car to stand near the two men.

Ian took her arm and said, "Let's get inside. I don't like you being out in the open like this."

She knew Ian just meant to guide her inside; he had no idea that the warmth of his hand through her flimsy sweater sleeve burned like a branding iron. Fire zinged along her nerve endings, and the initial attraction she'd felt for him earlier returned full force.

Shivering at another gust of freezing wind, she pulled away and headed for the door of the house. "I don't have a key." She'd left the ring on the end table along with her purse, having had no time to grab them before her flight from the house. Nor her coat. She reminded herself to get that before they left.

She reached for the knob just to see.

It twisted under her palm, and alarm zipped through her.

She stepped back—right into Ian's chest. His hands came up to rest on her goose-pimpled shoulders. "What's wrong?"

"It's unlocked."

She looked at Jase, who nodded. "Just to be on the cautious side, I climbed in the window you left open when you ran. There really wasn't any need, though. The guys were gone and didn't bother to lock the door when they left."

Gina wilted with relief as Ian grunted, "I'm surprised they closed it."

They entered the small foyer and Jase shut the door behind them. Destruction greeted her weary eyes. From the left to the right, debris had been strewn. Her purse had been dumped, but nothing appeared to be missing.

She walked into the den and felt despair sweep through her. Sighing, she said, "I had the door locked last night." She turned and looked at Ian. "I thought you would be here any minute but couldn't bring myself to leave it unlocked. Not after what happened the week before." She shuddered at the remembered terror of walking into her house and being threatened. She nodded to the door they'd just entered. "I heard the door squeak and for a brief moment, I thought it was you, then remembered I'd locked it." She gave a self-deprecating smile as she took in the chaos once more. "Guess a flimsy little lock like that wasn't going to keep them out, huh?" Her fingers worried the golden locket, still securely fastened around her neck.

Ian's hand came up and snagged hers, stilling the nervous habit. "Don't worry about it now. In the future we'll take more precautions."

We. She liked the sound of that. Perhaps too much.

Gina pulled her hand from his and laced her fingers together in front of her. "All right." She sighed. "I suppose the next step is to go through the house and figure out what they were looking for."

Jase gave her a look. "What about the police?"

"No, thanks. There's nothing they can do. These guys go higher than the police. And Mario specifically said not to go to them." She rubbed her weary eyes. "I just want to go through everything and see if anything looks—" she spread her hands, palms up, and shrugged "—whatever…suspicious? I don't know. I'm just praying I'll know it when I see it. I'm going to change into some warmer clothes, then get started."

Jase and Ian exchanged a look, then split up to help search.

Two hours later Ian slid another book on the shelf as Jason entered the study. "I need to talk to you about something."

Turning, fatigue gripping him, Ian dusted his hands against his jeans and looked at the man he'd once called friend. "What?"

Gina slipped into the room and sat behind the desk. Jase shot a pointed look in her direction and raised a brow at Ian. Ian looked at her and sighed. "You can talk in front of her. Whatever you know, she needs to know, too. These guys aren't playing around. Tell us what you found out."

Gina's appreciative glance warmed him even as he worried about what Jase had to say and how it might affect her.

Jason hesitated, then said, "I talked to several guys in the unit. Everyone is still together except you, me, Mario, Bandit and Les." Les Carson had been one of the team, a Ranger who'd taken a liking to Mario and had been one of Mario's best buds. As had Bandit McGuire.

"Where's Les?"

Jase rubbed his face and shut his eyes for a brief moment. "Dead. The official report says he was killed on a mission."

"The unofficial report?"

"He was arrested for treason and managed to hang himself in his cell."

Ian flinched. He hadn't heard this. How had he not known this? He looked back at Jase. Of course, the team would have covered for him to save his family from both the humiliation of having a traitor in the family and possible retaliation from those with a grudge against a man who would betray not just his country but also his team.

"What about Bandit?"

A shrug. "No one seems to know. He dropped off the edge of the earth about a year ago. If anyone knows where he is, no one's talking. Not even to me. He's either so deep undercover he'll never surface or he's dead and no one's talking about that either. I asked Mac about him and got shut up fast."

"And is Robbie Stillman still with Mac?"

"Yes. He took your place."

"That's what I heard."

"He's all right, I guess. Not the friendliest guy around but does a good job. I'd trust him with my back. Seems like he's got a lot of personal problems, though."

"Why are you helping us?" Ian stared hard at Jase, demanding a truthful answer, remembering his worry that he was trusting the wrong person.

Gina watched them from her seat behind the desk, quiet, almost invisible. Ian hadn't forgotten her presence, though.

Jason paced from one end of the den to the next. "When you called me, I wasn't sure if I should get involved."

"Again—why?"

"Because you and Mario were close, like brothers. Then you disappeared. And then Mario's behavior right before he died... It was so off."

"That's what you said. Can you think of anything more?"

"After one of our missions in South America, he seemed to withdraw from the rest of us. He would have surges of anger and would disappear for long periods of time…and other stuff. He even requested a leave of absence from the unit, but no one seems to know why."

"Was the leave granted?"

"No."

Ian frowned. "Why not?"

Jase shrugged. "I have no idea—he never said—but it was right before he died."

Gina intervened. "His grandmother died about a year ago. Maybe he was upset about that. He never really had time to process the loss. The day after her funeral he was deployed to a mission in Venezuela, I think."

"Could be—" Jase paced over to the bookshelf "—but like I said, the guys aren't talking much. There's something else going on and they're covering for him."

"What do you mean?"

"I mean the fact they all basically clammed up when I started asking questions about him. Makes me think it was possible he was into something he shouldn't have been and no one wants to be the guy to say anything about it."

The bad feeling in Ian's gut grew to mammoth proportions. "And you've no idea what it could have been?"

Jase hesitated once more, shot Gina another look then shook his head. "Not a clue."

Narrowing his eyes, Ian studied the man. Was he hiding something or did he just not want to say something in front of Gina? He'd get Gina out of the room in a minute and find out, but for now he followed Jase's line of thought. "Or, they could honestly not know anything to tell, especially if Mario was keeping his mouth shut because he didn't know who to trust."

"Yeah, that's possible, too."

"Hey, look at this," Gina exclaimed.

"What?" Ian strode to her side to look over shoulder. She had a Bible open on the desk. It was the piece of paper in her hand that had her attention.

"It's a letter from Mario."

The words were barely out of his mouth when the window shattered, glass flying. Gina screamed as Ian tackled her to the floor.

FIVE

A whimper escaped Gina and she bit her lip. Heart pounding, adrenaline rushing, she prayed as she shoved the letter into her pocket with a trembling hand. *God, what's going on?*

More gunshots sounded from outside, and she flinched at each report. Raising her head above the desk, she saw Ian crouched in front of the broken window, his gun pointed toward the darkness. He clipped off two more rounds. "Jase! Are you all right?"

Gina grabbed the phone from the desk and punched in 911. Then realized she had no dial tone.

Throwing the thing down, she scrambled across the floor and saw Jason on his back, blood flowing from a wound to his head.

"Oh, no," she whispered and worked her way to his side. She felt for a pulse. Strong enough to reassure her. "Okay, okay, Jase, you're going to be all right."

Ian fired another shot through the window, then turned to her. "We've got to get out of here."

"We can't just leave him!"

"Wouldn't think of it." He held up his cell. "I've already called for backup and an ambulance."

"What do we do until they get here?"

"Hold these guys off. Did Mario keep any guns around here?"

"I don't know. If he did, he never told me where they were."

A groan brought her attention back to the man on the floor. "Jase, Jase, can you get up?"

"My head," he moaned. "What happened?"

Another bullet pinged against the old fireplace. Gina ducked, although the bullet wasn't anywhere near her.

"You were shot, but I think it's just a graze," Gina whispered.

"Hey, buddy, you okay?" Ian asked as he kept his eyes on the action outside.

"Yeah. Yeah." He blinked and Gina watched his eyes slowly focus, although they stayed narrowed against the pain. "Where's my gun?"

Gina scanned the floor. "Over there."

With a wince, he shifted his weight and rolled to go into a position where he could reach the weapon. Then he weaved his way over to the window.

"You got a concussion?" Ian asked.

"Probably."

"I've got help up on the way, but I don't want to have to take the time to answer the questions I know they'll have. I hate to leave you but need to get Gina out of here."

"I'm all right. I've been hurt worse. Get Gina somewhere safe and let me know you're okay." He swiped at the blood trickling down the side of his face and turned back to the window.

Ian grabbed Gina's hand and pulled. She dug her feet in and repeated herself. "We can't just leave him!"

"Jase is a Ranger. He can take care of himself. It's up to me to take care of you. Plus, the cops will be here any minute. Once whoever's shooting at us hears those sirens, they'll disappear and Jase will have some help. He can hang on that long." A quick glance at his friend resulted in a nod of confirmation. "Now, please, let's move."

Gina caved and hurried after him with one last glance over her shoulder at Jase, who motioned for them to get out. Sirens sounded in the distance and relief flooded her. Hopefully the sound would scare off the attackers and Jase could get some help. "Go, go!"

Ian kept a tight grip on her hand as he led her toward the back of the house.

"What are we doing?" she gasped.

"Jase will handle the police. You and I are going to find someplace safe."

With a steady hand, Ian cracked the door leading to the outside and peered around it. The gunshots had ceased with the sound of the approaching sirens, but that didn't mean the bad guys were gone—it just meant they weren't shooting right now.

He scanned the area. All looked quiet. The car sat right where he'd left it. Untouched? Or a trap?

They'd have to chance it. Staying here meant talking to the police and having this take forever, trying to answer questions no one had the answers for and not knowing if they could be trusted anyway.

Hauling in a deep breath, he said, "Get in on this side. Duck low so you can't be seen from the other side of the car." He'd deliberately parked with the driver's side two feet from the bottom step of the small porch. On the opposite side of the car, at the end of the pier, the sounds of the ocean registered on a subconscious level.

Gina obeyed, crouching low, moving fast. Ian crawled in

right after her. Finally behind the wheel, he cranked the car and backed up the way he came in. "Stay down, Gina."

"I'm down. Won't the police stop us?"

"Nope."

Five seconds later, he was in front of the house. No gunshots split the air. A police car wheeled past him, then did a one-eighty to give chase.

"He's following us, Ian."

Her voice held a breathless, fearful quality that gripped his emotions. "I'll either lose him or Jase will radio the guy when he gets a chance and tell him to back off."

For ten minutes, the red and blue lights followed his every move; then they backed off and disappeared from view.

Ian relaxed a fraction and drove without a specific destination in mind. Gina straightened in her seat, groaning at protesting muscles.

"I have an idea," Ian offered.

"What?"

"I think I know a place we can hole up for a few hours to rest." He glanced at the clock.

"Where? I'm almost afraid wherever we go, they'll find us. How did they know to come back to the beach house?"

"Common sense. You didn't find what you were looking for the first time you were there, so it figures that you'd be back."

"So they were just waiting for us to show up? But why didn't Jase spot them?"

He shrugged. "Maybe they got there after Jase, spotted him and laid low to see how things would go down. Who knows?"

"Or maybe Jase called them," she whispered.

Indignation for the man welled up in him, and yet he couldn't deny a little niggling of doubt tickled his mind. "Jase wouldn't do that."

"Mario…"

"Mario should have let someone know what was going on and that he needed help."

"Maybe he did." She reached into her back pocket and pulled out the letter she'd found in the Bible.

Gina stared at the single sheet of paper containing Mario's slanting scrawl. She read aloud, "'Dear Gina, if you're reading this, I've failed. It wasn't my plan to die on you, darling, but as you well know, some plans are doomed from the get-go. I guess this was one of them.'"

"What plan?" Ian interrupted.

"Who knows?" She went back to reading. "'I've got some people after me. Really nasty guys. I've got something they want. If they haven't come after you yet, get ready. I'm sorry, Gina, I didn't want to do it this way but don't have time to come up with something better. Something that doesn't involve you. If I'm dead, they'll be looking for the next person who might know something, and whoever it is probably knows about you. I promise I did my best to hide your identity, but these guys are good; they'll find you, simply because I don't know who's involved. So, if they're going to come after you, I'm going to do my best to give you a fighting chance. I don't want to say what I've hidden, because if you know, you have no protection. If they catch you and you tell them, they'll kill you immediately. If you don't know, you can't tell them. That might buy you some time. I hope you've called Ian. If you haven't, do it. You're going to need him. I love you, Gina….'" Her throat clogged on the last part, and she stopped to take in a shuddering breath.

Ian clasped her hand, the warmth of his palm searing her,

giving her strength to finish the letter. "I'm sorry I didn't get the chance to show you how much. Ian's a good man. He'll know what to do. Grandmother thought the world of you. You're the only woman in her life who didn't disappoint her. Thank you for honoring her and keeping her memory close to your heart. All my love, Mario."

Silence filled the small rental. Tears dripped down Gina's chin as she scanned the letter through one more time.

Ian cleared his throat. Gina sighed.

"You…um…didn't have to read that out loud."

"I know, but if there's anything in there that can help us, you need to have the information."

"You were close to his grandmother. Did he have any other family?"

"No, just the sister who died. I suppose his mother is still out there somewhere, but…" She trailed off with a shrug and stared out the window. Time for a change of subject. "So, are you going to check on Jase?"

"Yeah." He dialed the number. Jase answered on the second ring. Ian asked, "Are you all right? What's the situation?"

"I've got it under control. I've also got a slight concussion but was lucky. I'm still alive."

Relieved, Ian said, "Good. Stay that way, will you? Listen, I'm going to take Gina someplace safe. I'll be in touch."

"Right. Let me know if you need anything. I'll keep digging into what Mario was doing before he died."

"Yeah, I'm going to do the same. Hey, what is it you wanted to tell me, but…couldn't earlier?" He let the question hang, hoping Jase would pick up on what he meant.

A pause. Then a sigh. "I think Mario was cheating on Gina." Shock and anger punched him, but Ian kept his voice steady. After all, he'd seen the possibility with his own eyes. He'd just wanted to chalk it up to the alcohol fogging Mario's brain at the time. "Why do you think that?"

"After a mission in Colombia, I saw him with a woman. They were looking pretty cozy."

"Probably just some undercover thing," he said, trying to justify it.

"No, we were done with the mission, coming down off the high that follows success."

"Huh. Then maybe…" He couldn't think of another excuse for Mario.

"I took some pictures of them."

That sparked some interest. "Why?"

"I don't know. Gina was such a great girl and it really bugged me that he would do something like that to her. I've been looking for a girl like her all my—" he cut himself off, but Ian felt a pang of sympathy for the man. "Anyway, I walked up and confronted him."

"In front of—"

"Yeah, in front of the girl."

Ian winced. "How'd that work out?"

"She got up and left. If her words had been a sword, Mario's head would have been rolling at her feet."

"Ouch."

"Aw, he deserved it. Anyway, I told him I had the pictures and if he ever did anything like that again, I'd give them to Gina."

"Whoa, Jase. Man, that was kind of…"

"I know, I know. Anyway, as you can imagine, Mario was furious. Threatened to kill me if I did anything to jeopardize his relationship with Gina. Told me to get rid of the pictures."

"Did you?"

Another pause. "No."

"See if you can figure out who the woman was."

"Will do."

"Great. Talk to you later." Ian hung up.

"So, what was that all about? Is Jase all right? And where are we going?" Gina's voice jerked his attention back to her.

He turned left, then a quick right. Ignoring the first question, he pointed. "There." Then he pulled to a stop in front of a gated home. "Jase is fine and handling the authorities beautifully. If he needs any more help, he'll call Mac." Then he nodded toward the house. "The guy that lives here is one of the best friends a guy could have, but best of all—he's got a top-notch security system."

SIX

Ian pulled up to the gated entrance and buzzed the house.

"Who lives here?" Gina asked.

"Nicholas Floyd. I can't believe he's actually home. He's a family court judge who made quite a bit of money in college when he designed a video game that shot to the best-seller chart and stayed there for years."

"A judge who designs video games?"

"Game. One."

"Seriously?"

"His passion is the law and helping others. He just happened to have an idea and the skills to implement it. Now he lives like this—and has an awesome security system."

"And he's your friend. Must be a God thing."

He smiled at her. "Must be." She was still as strong in her faith as she'd ever been. It was only one of the things he admired about her. "He had a death threat about a year and a half ago. Carly was the U.S. Marshal assigned to Nicholas and his family. Surprisingly enough they never met when Nick and I were roommates. Carly went to school out of state and Nick had his own family issues going on."

"Oh, wow. And he doesn't mind us just crashing his place?"

"Not at all. You'll understand once you meet him."

The twin gates separated at the middle and swung inward. Ian pressed the gas and drove through. The gates closed silently behind him. As he followed the winding drive up to the main house, he told Gina, "Nicholas and I roomed together in college for a couple of years. He's always loved the beach and swore he'd have an oceanfront home one day."

Gina gasped as the house came into view. It sprawled over the sloping hill, the picturesque ocean beating against the sand beyond. "It's beautiful."

Ian nodded. "He designed the house himself." The two-story brick structure sported white columned posts on the welcoming front porch. Four rockers surrounded a wrought-iron table, and a two-seater swing hung from the ceiling. Christmas lights were strung in massive amounts.

"I bet it's gorgeous at night, all lit up and just glowing."

A drawbridge began its smooth slow-motion descent until it gently touched the ground in front of the car.

Ian drove across. A quick glance behind her showed nothing there. No cars bearing men with guns, no popping sound of bullets connecting with metal and glass...

He parked in a small area to the right that had been designed to accommodate three cars. The other two slots sat empty.

Once out of the vehicle, Ian took her hand. "Nicholas is a great guy, but he's had a rather tragic life. I'll warn you, he's pretty much an extrovert personality, but he can be intense."

Okay, she could deal with intense. Intense had been her middle name lately.

But even Ian's warning didn't prepare her for the sight of the huge man who burst from the arched, double wooden front doors. At least six feet five inches tall, he was pure muscle, a tower of rock-solid strength. Before Gina could blink, he ran to Ian to embrace him in a bear hug, lifting Ian's feet off the ground. "Ian, my friend! How are you?"

Ian grunted, laughed and pulled out of the man's massive arms, protesting, "Nicholas, I told you not to do that. I'm fragile, man."

Nicholas punched Ian on the arm and turned to Gina. He'd turned so fast he hadn't seen Ian wince. But Gina did and she prepared to run should this mammoth decide to offer her the same type of embrace. Golden-green eyes stared down at her, studying her.

Then he gave a small bow and held out his hand.

Gina grinned at the knowing glint in his eyes and willingly shook his hand. Her fingers disappeared within his paw, and she felt like a toddler trying to play grown-up, shaking hands with the adult she'd just been introduced to.

"Nice to meet you, Mr. Floyd."

Shaking his head, he groaned. "I'm not that much older than you. Please, I'm Nicholas."

"Right. I'm Gina."

Those cat-green eyes narrowed, "And you're in trouble."

She immediately sobered. "Yes, but I don't want our coming here to place you in any danger."

For a brief moment a hard look flashed across his face. "Don't worry about it. I won't say this place is impenetrable, but no one will get in here without me knowing about it well beforehand. Long enough for us to either get out or get help. Okay?"

Ian stepped forward. "Don't worry, Gina. I wouldn't have brought you here if I thought it would endanger Nicholas or his family."

"Family?" she arched a brow.

"My mother, a niece and a nephew. And we don't have to worry about them. They're in Switzerland right now. I have a live-in cook and housekeeper, and they're specially trained in taking care of themselves, so…" An emotion glinted in his eyes but Gina couldn't put a name to it. Then he looked away from her and over at Ian. "How's that sister of yours?"

"Carly's great. I saw her just this morning. She offered to come stay with Gina last night to make sure the goons that are after her didn't get anywhere close. Thankfully, it was a peaceful night."

"Well, come on inside. Let's get you two settled. Do you have any luggage?"

Ian opened the trunk of his car and pulled out a small carry-on-size suitcase. "I have this, but Gina doesn't have a thing. Maybe your housekeeper could run out to the store to grab some things for us."

Those golden eyes tinged with green flecks turned back to her. "She's about Miriam's size. There's probably something inside she can use."

The three passed through the door and stepped into a large foyer. Antiques adorned the area and Gina sucked in an appreciative breath. "Your home is beautiful."

Nicholas swung his gaze back to her. "Thanks. I built it for my wife."

"Miriam?"

"Yes."

"Is she here?"

Ian cleared his throat and Gina looked at him. "Um, Miriam died about a year ago, Gina."

Sorrow coated her. "Oh, I'm so sorry."

Nicholas's gaze now held shutters. "I am, too. Thank you for your sympathy." Then he blinked and the grief was gone from him. "Now, let's see if we can get you comfortable. Stella! Where are you?"

Gina looked at Ian and mouthed behind Nicholas's back, "Stella?"

He shrugged.

Soon she had her answer. A tall, thin woman seemed to float into the foyer. She gave a quick glance to the visitors, then looked at Nicholas. "You bellowed?"

"Yes. I told you we'd be having visitors. Are the rooms ready?"

"Indeed. Follow me."

Nicholas spoke up. "After you get settled, you can use the conference room to work on whatever it is you need to work on. There's a computer with Internet access, a fax machine, the works. Help yourselves. I'm going back to study a difficult case I'm trying next week. Then we'll meet back up again for lunch. Is that all right with everyone?"

Ian nodded. "Do you have to be in court anytime soon?"

Those shutters descended over his eyes again. "No, I've taken some time off of other cases so I can work on this one right now. It's pretty intense." With an abrupt nod, he turned and exited the room.

Gina breathed a sigh of relief. As much as she appreciated this man's hospitality and safe haven, she wanted to get back to the whole reason she was here.

Finding out what it was someone wanted and who it was that wanted it.

Thirty minutes later, after a shower and a change of clothing, she emerged from her room and managed to locate the conference room, making only one wrong turn in the process.

She entered the room and took in the sight. It was very tastefully decorated. A cherry table dominated the center of the floor. Surrounding it were twelve comfortable office chairs.

Ian sat at one end, his nose buried in a file.

He looked up at her approach.

"What are you looking at?" she asked.

"I snitched a few things from the supply closet." He held up a notepad and pen. "I'm making notes on who to call, what we know, what we have questions about and where I think we might find the answers."

"An organization freak."

He grinned. "Some things never change."

"And some things do." She slid into the chair next to Ian.

He sobered. "Yeah, they do."

"What happened to Miriam?"

"She was killed in a car wreck."

"Ouch."

"Nicholas's sister, Janice, was with her. They were killed instantly."

"Oh, my. Is that why his niece and nephew live with him?"

"Yeah. They were staying with Nicholas's mother when the crash happened. A drunk driver."

"What about their father?"

"Janice was divorced. He left one day about five years ago and never came back, never called, nothing. It's like he disappeared from the face of the earth. I even tried finding him and had no luck. He has one other sister who has three children of her own and just couldn't take in more. Nick never hesitated in accepting the responsibility."

"Poor Nicholas."

"I know. But he's working through it, I think. It's hard to tell with him. Anyway, let's go over that note Mario left you. I feel like we're missing something here."

"Sure." She slid it from her pocket and took a deep breath. If they were missing something, she couldn't fathom what it might be.

Mario meant something by that note—Ian was sure of it. The man didn't do anything without a purpose, and if he'd taken the time to write a letter to Gina, he'd have made it mean more than what it looked like on the surface.

She spread the letter out before her and he watched a dark curl slip down to cover her left eye. He wanted to give it a tug so he could watch it spring back into place.

But he couldn't. He had to focus, find out who meant her harm. And what had Mario been doing the last few weeks of his life.

So, the first step. "Gina, the only way I'm going to be able to figure out what was going on with Mario is to do a full investigation, talk to the guys in the unit and our commanding officer, Mac Gold."

A frown furrowed her forehead. "But Mario thought one of them was a traitor. If you talk to them, how will you know that what they're telling you is the truth? I mean, if one of them had anything to do with Mario's death, he's not going to just come out and say so just because you're asking."

Ian rubbed a hand across his mouth and blew out a sigh. "I've got to be honest. I can't see any of those guys being a traitor."

Her gaze pierced him. "How long has it been since you've talked to them?"

Ouch. Okay, she had a point. "It's been a while. But—" he held up a finger "—I've talked to Mac on a regular basis since I left the unit. He and I have always been close, and he was the only one who didn't give me a hard time when I..." he murmured.

Gina looked away. "Yeah."

"Anyway, I'll give Mac a call and see if he has anything he can add to Mario's activities just before his death."

Worry had her fingering the gold locket. He watched her tug and twist on the fragile chain until he couldn't take it anymore. He reached over and covered her hand with his. "Relax, Gina. I'm going to take care of you."

Her eyes locked on his as her hand dropped from her throat. "Mario trusted you for some reason, in spite of the fact that he felt your leaving was a desertion of the unit. And I trust Mario.... At least I did." She stood and paced to the door. Hand on the knob, she turned back. "So, I guess that means I have to trust you by default. Please don't make me regret it."

SEVEN

Four hours later, having nibbled on a turkey sandwich and chips provided by his host's cook, Ian sat back and rubbed his burning eyes. He'd checked on Gina right after lunch, and she'd been stretched across her bed, sound asleep.

Ian had decided to let her catch up a bit on her rest and returned to his phone calls and information gathering. Unfortunately, he'd not managed to acquire much of anything new, a fact that left him feeling frustrated and helpless. Tossing his pen down on the notepad, he groaned out loud and stood to pace over to the window.

Waves crashed silently beyond the other side of the glass as the sun dipped to touch the water.

It had been a long day.

And they still didn't know much.

"Hey."

He turned with a start to find Gina standing in the doorway blinking away remnants of sleep. He fought the urge to go to her and pull her into his arms. Instead, he cleared his throat and asked, "Do you feel better?"

She stepped into the room and gave a pointed glance to the paperwork in front of him. "Yes, if a bit guilty that you've been working all this time."

He waved away her concern. "It's fine. You've had a few stressful moments lately. You needed the sleep."

A crooked smile curved her lips. "Yes, *stressful* would be a good word." She slipped into the chair next to him, close enough for him to catch a whiff of the scent that was uniquely her—a mix of cinnamon and some kind of spice. She smelled like Christmas. He concentrated on her words.

"So, I take it you've made a few phone calls."

"A few." He nodded.

"What did your old commanding officer, Mac, have to say?"

"That he knew of a few things Mario was working on but would have to get back to me. He was taking a short break to visit his son."

"His son?"

"Yeah, Jimmy."

"I've known Mac for a while now. How did I not know he had a son?" She tried to remember if the subject had ever come up.

Ian looked up at her. "It's not something he talks about a lot. Jimmy's twenty-five or -six now and lives in an adult group home. He's a mentally challenged adult. Down syndrome, I think."

Gina asked indignantly, "Is he ashamed of him?"

"No, that's not it. I think he just feels guilty that he doesn't spend more time with him. And talking about it reinforces that fact. So he just…doesn't say anything."

"Amazing."

"What?"

"That you can know someone and—not know them."

"In addition to not spending a whole bunch of time with him, I think Mac also feels a little guilty about putting Jimmy in the home. His marriage fell apart then when his ex died a few years ago, he didn't have any relatives stepping up to help out and he still had to make a living…." He shrugged.

"Poor Mac."

"Jimmy's fine. The home is some swanky ranch-type place where they have a lot of animals for the clients. Jimmy's happy and I think Mac made the right decision. He thinks he did, too, and is getting used to the idea. But he goes out there just about every chance he gets to visit."

"So, that's where he is now." She spread her hands, palms up. "We hurry up and wait?"

"Something like that."

Gina blew out a sigh and pulled out a piece of paper. Laying it on the table, she smoothed it out, pressing it, running her fingers over the crinkles.

Ian raised a brow. "Is that the letter?"

"Yes." She kept her gaze on the words in front of her.

"Do you mind if I look at it?"

She lifted sad eyes to his. "No, I don't mind." She passed it over to him, her fingers grazing his as he took the letter from her. Emotion speared him at the brief touch. His gaze held hers. "I'm not a traitor, Gina, no matter what you think."

She blinked but didn't break eye contact. "It doesn't really matter what I think. Mario trusted you in the end, so that's all that matters."

Raw grief nearly cut him in two, and the strength of it shocked him. He wanted to tell her why he had left, wanted to with everything in him, but…now wasn't the time.

She might not believe him anyway.

And the truth might send her running from him, which would cause a whole new set of problems.

Like how he would keep her safe if she refused to be around him.

No, he'd wait to tell her his heart. Possibly forever.

Time passed slowly for Gina as they worked on trying to discover what Mario had been up to right before his death. Ian spent every waking moment on the laptop or the phone Jase had delivered to him, and Gina knew he was desperately searching for any information on Mario.

The next day, they finally caught a break. Mac Gold called with news about something Mario had been working on.

Ian activated the speakerphone button so Gina could listen in, too.

"Go ahead, Mac. I've got Gina here with me."

A heavy sigh sounded over the line and Gina shot Ian a worried look. He covered her hand with his, and she sucked in a breath at the unexpected contact. But her heart warmed at his attempt at comfort. She gave a tremulous smile and turned her attention to Mac's words.

"Look, it's not pretty and I can't confirm a lot of it—yet. But it looks like Mario was working on some kind of a gun-running investigation."

"I don't understand," Gina broke in. "You were his commanding officer. Wouldn't you know what he was working on?"

A slight pause. "Not if he was doing something on his own."

Ian closed his eyes and rubbed them. "All right, so he got some information about gun runners, then possibly went undercover to make sure it was right. They caught on to him and tried to kill him, but he got away long enough to put Gina's life in danger. But why wouldn't he ask for help? That's the part I don't get. Why wouldn't he bring the team in on it?"

"I don't have the answer to that question. But you do have a reasonable theory. However, it could be that somehow he was involved with these guys, made them mad about something, possibly took something that didn't belong to him, and now they're after it."

"Mario wouldn't betray his country, Mac." The steel in Ian's voice surprised Gina. The man truly didn't believe Mario would do anything illegal. Relief flooded her. She so wanted Mario to be innocent of any wrongdoing.

Mac's voice echoed through the room. "I don't want to believe it either, Masterson, but I don't have enough proof to go either way. He wasn't under my command with what he was found to be investigating. That raises a red flag for me."

"Right." Ian sighed and said, "What did the others in the unit have to say? Did they tell you anything more?"

"Not much. Just confirmed what I just told you. I did all this via phone, since I'm still out here with Jimmy. I'll be back in my office in a few hours, and I'll be able to keep pressing from there. I'll talk to each of my men face-to-face but don't know that I'll be able to turn up much of anything else."

"Okay, thanks, Mac. Tell Jimmy I said hello."

"Will do. Good luck and call if you need anything. I'll be in touch."

They hung up and Ian turned to Gina. "What do you think? Does any of that ring a bell?"

She shook her head and shifted in her chair. "No, none of it. But that doesn't surprise me. Mario would never share details of a case with me. Ever. Not even when I asked."

Ian rubbed his chin. "No, he wouldn't. Of course he wouldn't. All right, then, let me show you one more thing I did."

"What?"

She leaned in closer while he tapped on the keys of the

laptop in front of him and breathed in his clean scent. He'd taken the time to shower.

You're not here to notice how good he smells. Focus.

Ian brought up a series of letters and numbers on the screen. "I accessed my high-security clearance account and input the letter Mario left you. I was looking for some kind of code."

"A code?"

"Sure, we come across them all the time in our line of work. It wouldn't have been any trouble for Mario to come up with one off the top of his head and leave it for you to find. Plus, you know how he loved puzzles and such. I wouldn't put it past him to do something like that."

"Okay. And?"

"And nothing. I ran it through the military-grade software for code breaking, so to speak, and nothing."

"So what does that mean?"

"It means that the letter is just…a letter."

"So, no code?"

"Nope, no code. Unless it's in the wording and something only you can understand. Which is what I've thought from the very beginning. So the ball's back in your court. It's up to you to find any hidden meanings in Mario's words."

She took the letter from his outstretched hand, this time careful to make sure she had no contact with him. The knowing look in his eyes made her flush, but she ignored it and her reaction to him by looking down at the familiar handwriting. Guilt pierced her. Here she was trying to elude someone who wanted her dead, working on figuring out what her fiancé had been up to, and she found herself attracted to a man Mario had actually cursed.

Gina stood and walked to the door. "All right. I'll just, um, take this back to my room and study it some more." Which would be a waste of time, since she had the thing memorized at this point, but she needed to escape and it was as good enough an excuse as any other she might try to come up with.

"Right, you do that. After supper, Nicholas has volunteered to go over some of this with me tonight and see if his fresh eyes can spot something mine can't."

"Go over what?" She paused, hand on the doorknob.

"He going to dig into some legal stuff, court cases and bad guys that Mario helped bust. He had an idea that whoever is after you might be a family member, or something, of someone Mario either, um, killed or put in jail."

Darkness seemed to shroud her for a moment. "I know something was haunting him, something that just wouldn't leave him alone…. And he didn't know what to do with it."

Ian stood and avoided her eyes. "Yeah, we all have stuff like that."

Gina retraced her steps back across the room to touch his arm. "I'm sorry, Ian." Then she left and made her way to her bedroom, her thoughts racing, the words from Mario's letter burning in her mind.

What could he have meant? She flopped onto the bed, ignored her growling stomach, and studied it one more time. What kind of message could he have hidden in this straightforward-sounding letter?

Line by line she went through it again. Time passed as she concentrated, trying to put new meaning to the words.

Nothing. She closed her eyes and tried putting a picture with each line in the letter. Tried to visualize it.

"Close to your heart. Keep her close to your heart. Close to…"

Her hand flew to her throat in sudden realization. She

grabbed the necklace, held it in her suddenly unsteady fingers, and wondered. Could it be?

It had to be.

Practically tumbling from the bed, she got her feet under her and raced for the door.

"Ian! Ian, I've got it!"

EIGHT

Ian heard her yell and bolted from the conference room. They rounded the corner at the same time, sending her crashing against his chest. His arms came up protectively and held her tight.

Or tried to.

She scrambled back but grabbed his forearms and said excitedly, "It's the locket."

"What?"

She grabbed the necklace around her neck and pulled it out for him to see. "The locket. The letter. The clue. Oh, come on." She dragged him back into the room and fiddled with the clasp on the chain, trying to release it. Finally, she dropped her hands and said, "I can't get it. Can you?"

Gina pulled her ponytail up and off her neck and Ian swallowed hard. With hands that held a slight tremble and a sudden propensity to sweat, he told himself to get a grip. This had to do with Mario. She'd figured something out.

"This is pretty heavy. Doesn't it hurt your neck to wear it?"

She gave a shaky chuckle. "No, I guess I'm used to it. Mario loved to see it on me, and I finally just quit taking it off except at night. You wouldn't believe the compliments I get."

Finally the hook released and the necklace wilted into her

palm. She sat at the table and with shaky hands managed to hold on to the locket while she slid a thumbnail between the edges to open it.

A younger version of Mario stared back at them from one side, and a girl of about ten years old from the other.

Gina traced a finger over the pictures. "This is Mario's sister, Patrice. She died on a mission trip in South America when she was sixteen."

"Yeah, he told me about her. I remember he was torn up about it. She and two others were killed in some kind of cross fire between guerrillas and the Colombian military."

"He never got over it," she murmured.

Impatience crawled through him. "Okay, so how does this tie in with what was in Mario's letter?"

She frowned. "In the letter, he said, 'Thank you for keeping her memory close to your heart.' So, it got me thinking that maybe he meant this…that there was something more than just keeping her memory alive…. What if he meant…" She held the locket up to the light, squinting at the piece of gold metal. "Something…like…this…right here. Does it look like it opens again?"

He took it from her. "Maybe. Some kind of secret compartment?"

"Exactly. Can you get it open?"

"Yes, hold on one second. Look, it's a little switch." He pressed it and the bottom opened up.

A small key fell out and Gina gasped. "You found it."

He smiled at her. "No, you found it." He studied the small item. "Now we just have to figure out what it goes to."

Racking her brain, Gina paced the floor of the conference room. "I don't know, Ian. The first thing that comes to mind is a safe-deposit box."

He nodded as he examined the key, turning it one way then another. No identifying marks stood out. He looked up at her. "You're right. That's exactly what it is. Mario would expect you to know what it was to if he hid it in the necklace."

"Yes, he would. Okay—" she shrugged "—it's got to be where he banked."

"So, we'll call and find out if he's got a box there."

"Um, I don't know which bank. I know he had accounts at two different ones. One in Georgia where he was stationed at the base and one in Spartanburg."

He looked at the clock. "It's too late to call today—they're closed. We'll try first thing in the morning."

"Okay." Out of habit, she touched the spot below her throat where the locket usually rested. Ian was looking at her hand. She followed his gaze, wondering if she had dirt or something on it. "What?"

"Huh?" His eyes snapped up to hers.

"You've got a funny look on your face. What?"

He reached out and took her hand in his. Heat zipped through her arm and up into her neck. Why did he affect her so? She focused on his words. "You're not wearing your ring."

Gina snatched her hand away and clasped it with her other. "No. I took it off." She stalked back to the window.

"Why?"

She tossed her hands up. "What does it matter?"

He shrugged, "I guess it doesn't, but it just struck me as odd."

She stamped a foot. "Oh, if you must know, I took it off in a fit of anger. When all this started and I couldn't figure out what was going on. Then I realized Mario had done something to lead these guys to me…" she swallowed hard. "I was mad at him. Mad at him for whatever he'd gotten himself into, mad at him for getting himself killed—and mad that he left me to deal with the fallout." Ian looked stunned at her outburst, yet understanding flitted across his face.

Abruptly, she spun around and said, "I've got to call my parents. They've probably already called my brother, Joseph, and reported me missing—and I can just imagine what he thought when he saw my house…. Plus, I need to warn them…." She trailed off and sucked in a deep breath. "They need to be cautious. I didn't call them before because I didn't want the people after me to think that they might know where I was…. But I just can't stand the thought of them worrying about me."

He thought about it a minute. "You're right to be careful. But Joseph's FBI. He can take care of himself—and your family. You should call him and he can decide what to tell your parents, if anything. Here, use the encrypted cell."

She took the phone from his outstretched hand and gave him an embarrassed smile. She should have just said she'd taken the ring off and left it at that. Grateful that he let her get away with the topic change, she said, "Thanks."

Thirty seconds later she had her brother, Joseph, an FBI agent in her hometown of Spartanburg, South Carolina, on the phone.

He wasn't happy. "Gina? Where are you? What's going on? I went to your place and it was trashed! Why didn't you call me?"

She held the phone a few inches from her ear. Ian's raised eyebrow indicated that he had no trouble hearing Joseph's explosion.

"Breathe, Joseph. Calm down."

"Calm down? I get a call from Dad that no one's seen or heard from you in days and you tell me to calm down?

We've got a missing persons report filed with the police department, and Mom's just about ready for a straitjacket. Don't you tell me to calm down!"

She winced. "I'm sorry. I should have called earlier, but I was afraid the people after me might…" She blew out a breath. "Look, I've…run into some trouble."

"And you don't think I might have been the person you should have called? Why *didn't* you call me?" His growl rumbled through her and she paused. Why hadn't she called Joseph? She looked at Ian leaning back in the comfortable leather chair. He made no effort to hide his interest in the conversation.

"Because Mario told me to call Ian Masterson."

"Ian? Ian? The dude who deserted his unit? The one Mario was so furious with? And how—and when—did Mario tell you to call Ian?"

Gina blew out a sigh. It did sound bad when he put it that way. "It's a long story, but yeah—that one. And he told me…"

"Look, never mind. Where are you?" he interrupted.

"I can't tell you."

Gina braced herself for another eruption; then Ian took the phone from her hand.

"This is Ian. I'll be taking care of the situation."

She watched, stupefied, as Ian smoothly handled her brother and his worried insistence that he come to help. In the end Ian won, reassuring Joseph that he had everything under control and saying he would call if he thought Joseph could help.

Gina cleared her throat when Ian hung up the phone with a bemused smile on his face. She shrugged. "He loves me."

"Trust me, I know the feeling."

She blinked. "Huh?"

He flushed as he realized what he'd implied. "I have a sister, too, remember?"

Her face flamed. "Oh, right. Carly. Yes. Well. Um…"

Ian grinned at her and she threw her hands up.

And the laughter rolled out of both of them.

When they caught their breath, Gina looked up at him. 'It really wasn't that funny."

"Maybe not, but I needed the laugh."

She sobered. "Yeah, better take it while you can."

Who knew when the next opportunity for a good belly laugh would present itself, given their current circumstances?

"Gina." The whisper and a rough shake of her shoulder jerked her out of a sound sleep. Terror shot waves of panic through her as a scream clawed to the top of her throat. A hand covered her mouth and blackness greeted her eyes. For a minuscule second she flashed back to the moment she'd stepped into her house and the blindfold had been slapped on her face. Now she struggled and tried to scream but nothing escaped the rough palm clamped over her lips, rough fingers digging into her cheek.

She couldn't breathe!

Her heart fluttered like a butterfly held by one wing. Gathering her wits, she struggled against the grip, then whimpered as a large head descended toward her.

"Shh." The whispered warning rolled from her like water from a duck. Fear overwhelming her, she continued her useless attempts to escape her captor.

He said again, "Gina, shh. Be quiet."

His voice penetrated her fog of horror. Then she smelled his familiar scent. Peppermint.

Ian.

She ceased all movement and went limp against his han He moved it and said in a voice so soft she almost did catch it, "Follow me."

"What's wrong?" Instinct made her whisper. Then s punched his arm—hard enough to make her wince at t pain that shot up from her knuckles. "Did you have to sca me to death?"

"I'm sorry. I couldn't take a chance on you screamin when I woke you up. Someone's breached securit Nicholas's taking care of things on his end, but I've got get you out of here. Now, no more questions until we'r safe, okay?"

The fear she'd felt only moments before returned in tri licate. "Right." A quick glance at the bedside clock told he it was 3:00 in the morning.

She slipped from beneath the covers, thankful she'd dresse in sweats. "I need shoes."

A sound outside the door had him hurrying her eve faster. "No time."

So, once again, she would be making a run for it barefoot "Why don't I hear an alarm going off?"

"It's a silent alarm. Now, hush."

She hushed and held tight to his warm hand, following closely on his heels. She had no idea how they would ge out of the house without running into whoever had tripped the alarm, but she'd just have to trust Ian to keep her safe.

He led her away from the door where they'd heard noise and out of the second door that led into the hall, gun gripped in his right hand, funny-looking glasses now covering his eyes.

Night vision goggles. Of course.

Another right turn. A left.

Then he abruptly turned and pulled her into the room to the right.

Her breath came in pants; her heart thundered in her ears so loudly she was sure Ian could hear it. And where was Nicholas? Was he in danger? Were the cops on the way?

As if in answer to her question, sirens sounded in the distance.

Ian easily made out the figure at the end of the hall just before he pulled Gina into the room behind him. A pro. Dressed in army fatigues—and an M16 assault rifle held comfortably in his hands.

One of his own? Another Ranger? Dread crawled through him. These guys were serious. *Mario, what have you done?*

Gina shifted behind him and he could hear her desperately trying to quiet her breathing. Fortunately, the bad guy was far enough away that he couldn't hear her.

Okay—Ian thought quickly, new plan.

He looked around. The balcony. Motioning for Gina to stay put, he scurried over to look out. A tree stood close enough, and if he were by himself, he'd be over the rail and down the tree in minutes. However...

He looked over at the scared woman, trembling where he'd left her—yet with a look in her eyes that said she'd go down fighting.

Good. She'd need that spirit. He moved back to the door and listened. Footsteps sounded to his left. Soon they'd be here to search this room.

He grabbed her hand and pulled her toward the balcony. In shock, she noticed it was raining. Sometime during the night, the clouds had released their burden. Leaning next to her ear, he whispered, "How are you at climbing?"

Fear shot through her eyes, but she shrugged it off "Guess we're going to find out."

He looked at the limb, then the ground below. "Hold on."

Racing back into the room, he shifted the pack on his back and snatched a sheet from the bed. He pulled a knife from his belt, making a cut in the middle of the sheet, then ripped it into a long thick strip. With swift, sure movements, he tied one end around his waist.

Back on the balcony with Gina, he tied the other end around her. "Okay, I'm going to go first. Once I'm in the tree, I can help you over and down, got it?"

She nodded, never taking her midnight eyes from his. Trust shone in their depths. Trepidation filled him. *Oh, God, don't let me let her down.*

Then he was over the railing and reaching for the tree limb, blinking against the blinding downpour. Once he had a secure hold on it, he swung himself over and onto it. Gina already had one leg over the side of the balcony, her eyes on something back in the room.

Were they already in there?

She scrambled over to the edge, her fingers reaching— and not quite long enough to grasp the limb.

"You'll have to jump, Gina."

She gasped and turned to look behind her. Whirling back, one hand still on the rail, she took a deep breath and leaped toward the limb. Her fingers curled around the branch, her weight pulling on Ian.

A loud crack echoed through the night and Ian flinched, thinking they'd been spotted and shot at.

Then he felt the limb shift and dip.

Gina eyes went wide, then blinked repeatedly as the rain poured onto her face. Sputtering, she swallowed hard, still dangling from the tree like a child getting ready to work the monkey bars.

"Don't move," Ian whispered. He glanced at the doors on the balcony and could see shadowy figures casing the room. Soon, they'd be out on the balcony.

And he and Gina would be trapped.

NINE

Gina gripped the branch and felt every muscle in her shoulders start to scream in protest. As quickly as the rain seemed to have started, it lightened to a drizzle. The limb fell slack against her palm. The cold seeped in. "Ian, I'm going to fall," she whispered.

"No, you're not. I won't let you. You're tied to me, remember?"

She gave a watery, humorless puff of a chuckle that came out sounding like more of a grunt. The terror shuddered inside her in spite of Ian's reassuring presence and highly trained skills. "That simply means if I fall, you do, too."

"Just," he grunted, "give me one more second."

"What are you doing?"

"Getting you off that limb. Okay, I'm wedged in here, now start coming my way, inch by inch. Now that I'm off the limb, maybe it'll hold for you."

"Maybe?" she squeaked.

"Move, Gina, we don't have much time."

She moved. Slowly, ever so slowly, she worked her way over to the sound of his voice. The limb gave another groaning creak and she froze.

Ian's whisper reached her. "Don't stop now—you're almost here."

She kept going—until she lost her grip. One hand slipped off and she dangled like a monkey, cramped fingers holding on for dear life, the other arm windmilling, trying to grab back onto the limb. A whimper escaped her.

Then a hard hand clasped her flailing wrist and Ian hauled her the rest of the way over and up against his chest's rapidly beating heart.

She stood there, shivering, arms clasping the man who was determined to keep her safe and scare her to death all in one night.

"Ready?"

They still had to get down the tree to the ground—then somehow get to the car.

Suddenly, the cold air hit her and she couldn't stop shaking. How would she make it down the tree? It seemed as if an hour had passed since they'd started this run for their lives, yet in reality she knew it had been only minutes.

"Okay. I'm ready," she gasped.

"Follow me."

He started the trek down the tree, one foot gently placed, the other following. Slowly, they worked their way down. Just as they touched the ground, the balcony door opened above them and a uniformed body leaned over the railing. He paused, spotted them, then mimicked Ian's initial move.

He jumped for the tree.

When he hit the limb, it gave another booming snap— and man and limb fell two stories to crash at the base of the tree.

Ian grasped her hand and pulled her after him, her bare feet tickled by the rain-drenched yard and nearly frozen stiff as the cold wind blew across her. She looked back to see the man lying there, not moving. Was he dead?

There was no time to find out.

Ian led her to the edge of the moat and without hesitation, hit the water, yanking her after him.

The cold wetness came to her waist and nearly sucked the air from her lungs. Her knees buckled but she pressed on and within seconds was out on the other side, dripping water and shivering like someone struck with a seizure. "Wh-wh-what now?" she stuttered.

Ian pulled a set of keys out of his sopping pants. "Get in."

He'd moved the car. To the other side of the moat.

"You planned for this?" She crawled in, not worrying about soaking the seat; she just wanted to get away.

"I used to be a Boy Scout."

Slamming the door, she grabbed the seat belt. Intuition told her this might be a rough ride.

Ian started the car, backed up, put the vehicle in Drive— and came nose-to-nose with headlights. "Duck down!"

Slamming the car into Reverse, he skidded backward, flinging the wheel to the right, then the left.

Then back into Drive.

Gina lifted her head as the wheels squealed on the concrete. "What about the gate?" she panted.

"My guess is it's open—just in case they needed to get out quick. If not, I'll have to figure something else out."

A minute later his guess proved true. The gates stood wide, beckoning them into the darkness beyond. Ian sped through.

"They're behind us, Ian." Her heart pounded in her chest, fear clogging her throat. "How did they know where we were? How did they get past Nicholas's security?"

Ian reached over and turned the heat on full blast. "All

good questions that will have answers later. Right now I need to drive. We also need warm clothes and a place to hole up."

A bullet shattered the rear window, and Gina swallowed a scream as she ducked lower. "Ian?"

"Just hold on. I know this part of Myrtle Beach like the back of my hand. I'll lose them in a few minutes."

Another shot rang out and a thump sounded in the rear of the car, and Gina prayed as Ian spun the wheel and took the turn for the interstate.

Beside him, Gina shivered uncontrollably; Ian knew he needed to do something fast about clothing. They couldn't stay in their thin pajamas. Even with the heater blowing wide open, the cold felt as though it had already seeped through to his bones. She stuttered through chattering teeth, "A-a-are they still behind us?"

"No, I think I managed to lose them." He'd gone on a wild ride of twists and turns, back roads, then on the highway, then off again, calling Mac and Jase in for reinforcements. "I grabbed my pack with a lot of essentials in it, but nothing much to change into. If we're fast, we can get a change of clothing and find a hotel so we can plan our next move."

"There's always an open-all-night tourist store along this road. What about stopping at one of those?"

"Fine, but it'll have to be a hit-and-run thing. Grab something, pay for it and get out."

An hour and a half later, satisfied he'd lost whoever had been chasing them, he pulled into a small oceanfront town on the outskirts of Myrtle Beach, South Carolina, and found a store.

Pacing from one end of the wooden storefront porch to the other, he checked his watch. He'd handed her a handful of cash and Gina had disappeared into the open-all-night store five minutes ago. He'd done his best to hide the car in the darkness of the little alley that ran alongside the store, but it wasn't very deep, holding trash cans and other debris blocking his way. He'd just have to pray it would be enough.

Headlights appeared in the distance, amping his adrenaline up a notch.

He slid deeper into the shadows of the wooden porch. If those were the guys after Gina, they'd probably recognize the car.

Of course, if the make and model didn't clue them in, the missing window in the back and several bullet holes around the right taillight probably would—if they saw the car. He prayed they'd miss it.

But if they didn't...

Already-tight shoulders hardened into granite.

"I'm ready," Gina's breathless voice came from behind his left ear. "I got you some sweats, socks and shoes, too."

Keeping his eyes on the approaching vehicle, he said out of the corner of his mouth, "Step behind me and stay out of sight."

"What is it?" He felt her move without hesitation even as she asked the question, the warmth of her hand resting on the small of his back. He ignored the zing up his spine as a result of her touch and focused on the car. How had they been found? He knew he'd lost those who were chasing them and lost them good. There was no way they should have caught up with them this fast. Unless...

They'd planted something on the car.

Ian mentally slapped his head. He should have thought of that. It's what he would have done, but even if it had occurred to him, as fast as they'd had to leave Nicholas's, he would have had no time to sweep the car anyway. Chilled inside and out, Ian realized these guys were good—maybe better than he. They'd seen the car on their way into Nicholas's and planted the tracker just in case.

A precaution that had paid off for the bad guys.

More questions hit him. Then again, if they'd planned to kill them in the house, why had they planted a tracking device? Why not just dismantle it? Had they wanted them to get away?

Ian took the bag of clothes from her hand—and the lead—and pulled her along behind him at a fast clip through the parking lot. Christmas brought loads of people to the beach for the lights and just the pleasure of spending the holidays on the water. Fortunately, even at this late hour, there were a fair number of people and cars all around them. Probably due in part to the all-night bar open two doors down.

One store led to the next. Staying in the shadows proved to be nearly impossible in the well-lit areas they had to pass through in order to get to the next building. As a result, they hurried, heads ducked, Ian on the outside.

She suddenly realized why he'd done that. He was protecting her. A bullet would have to go through him to get to her.

Something to think about later.

Ian jerked her arm and she found herself in another alley, her back against the wall, with Ian's hand pressed over her mouth. Startled, she stared up into those electrifying blue eyes. He removed his hand and placed a finger against his lips in the universal symbol for silence.

She nodded.

Satisfied she'd stay quiet, he moved away and for a moment she felt bereft. His large presence made her feel safe, protected.

But she couldn't rely totally on him. She had to use her

brain, stay calm, keep her terror under control. Because if she didn't, she'd make some stupid mistake that could get her—and Ian—killed.

He returned, his jaw tight, eyes narrowed.

"What is it?" she asked.

"They're gone. They must have decided they'd lost us."

She blinked. "Do you think they'll be back?"

"Maybe. I'm hoping they've given up for the night."

"Do you think they found your car?"

"No doubt. I feel sure they put a tracking device on it. And they're going to realize because of where I parked it, we deserted it and are now on foot. They'll regroup and form a plan on how to find us." He looked back over at the car. "I'm sure they searched that vehicle, though, which is why I've got to call the police and report this. If they left any kind of evidence behind, a strand of hair, anything, I want it documented. We need crime-scene people out here. Not only because the rental company would have it investigated anyway, but also because it'll give us the protection of a distraction."

Fear immediately swamped her as the only word that registered was *police*.

Her fingers reached up to toy with the heavy locket she'd placed back around her neck. "No, you can't. It's not the police I'm really worried about—it's the fact that once they've finished their part, they'll turn it over to the army to investigate. And I think that'll cause more problems than we want." She shook her head. "And I know for a fact that Mario didn't want the army investigating this."

"All right." He blew out a breath. "Then I'll call Mac back. He can handle this himself, but we're not hanging around. We're getting out of here before those guys come back."

"And you're positive you can trust Mac?"

"He's the best option we've got right now. The man knew Mario, had a lot of respect for him."

"I know. He was a pallbearer at the funeral," she whispered.

"Yeah, I saw him."

She thought about that day, the look on his face when she'd turned and walked away without a word. "I didn't expect to see you there."

Pain darkened his blue eyes to stormy seas. "Of course I would be there. He was my friend."

Gina swallowed and looked away. "I know he was. I'm sorry." She was also sorry for the way she'd treated him that day. He'd been hurting, too, in spite of the fact that she'd believed him to be something akin to a traitor.

He closed his eyes for a brief moment. "Me, too."

"All right, I trust you. Call him if you think that's what we need to do."

"I think it is."

Within minutes, Ian had his former commanding officer on the phone and explained their current situation. He hung up and turned to her. "He'll be out here shortly. He said to get out of sight while he contacts the local police and requests a crime-scene unit to be dispatched to go over the car. I'm reporting it as a civilian. I've kept your name out of it. Mac will, too."

Worry filled her. She prayed it was the right thing to do.

"All right. But won't the police wonder why this car was shot up and where we went?"

"Yep, but I'm not going to worry about that right now. I've put in a request to my supervisor allowing me to be assigned to finding the people responsible."

"And they're going to let you do that?"

"It's either that or I continue my personal leave. I have

about ten weeks' worth I can use. Don't worry about it, Gina. I'm going to take care of it, all right?"

She hated to admit he was right. Qualified and willing, he could do a much better job of catching the bad guys than she. And yet, she knew that for however long it took to figure out what Mario had been involved in and catch the people after her, she'd be right in Ian's back pocket. No way was she going to just sit meekly in a hotel room, waiting for someone to come through the door shooting. And she sure couldn't go home and put her family in danger.

"All right, but I'm sticking with you, okay?"

He raised a brow. "We'll see. Now let's find a place to change."

Ian didn't know how much of Gina's "closeness" his heart would be able to handle. On the other hand, he couldn't deny he wanted to be near her. And yet, if the gunmen returned—and he had almost no doubt that they would—he didn't want her in the line of fire.

Looking at the stubborn set of her jaw, he figured he might have to get creative on that end.

Impatience clawed at him. They needed to get out of here, out of the open. He felt exposed, yet they couldn't leave just yet. Mac wanted to see the crime scene, and Ian needed to see Mac. The man was bringing him more gear and information on Mario's cases, and Ian wasn't leaving without that stuff.

A car pulled up and a face from the past materialized before him. Mackenzie Gold climbed out of his black F-150 pickup truck. The years hadn't been good to the man, who now sported a full head of gray hair and more wrinkles than a pug, but he hadn't lost his rigid military bearing or piercing green eyes. Ian stepped out of the shadows and held out a hand. "Thank you for coming out, sir."

"You're still one of my men, Masterson, transfer or no." He looked around, uneasiness reflected on his face. "Let's move over toward the car. I want to see it." His eyes flicked up the road and back. "But let's make this quick. I don't like being out in the open like this." He ushered them back over to the mangled car, where the crime scene unit was already working. "Roadblocks are set up so no one uses this road until we're done. Hello, Gina." He gestured toward Gina as he handed over the bag to Ian.

"Mac." She eyed him and gave him a tight smile.

The commanding officer turned his attention back to Ian. "Here's the folder with everything I could dig up on Mario." He handed him a flash drive. "More information I copied. Some of this is classified." He shot Ian a ferocious look. "Destroy that when you're done with it, and if you get caught with it, you didn't get it from me."

Ian nodded his thanks and pocketed the drive. He stuck the folder under his armpit and said, "I don't know what Mario was doing, but we're going to find out."

Gina spoke up, "It seems like Mario had something the men who did this want and they think I've got it."

"Do you?"

"That's the problem. I don't know, but we're figuring that out."

"What do you have?"

Ian intervened. "Unfortunately, she doesn't have a clue what they could be after. I've left out a few details in my report to the cops. I'd appreciate it if you'd go along with it if anyone asks. Now we're getting out of here. I don't know where those guys are, but I want to put some distance between us and them."

"You got it." He pierced Ian with those direct eyes. "Keep me updated. I can't help you if you leave me in the dark. I'll do the same for you."

"Absolutely, sir."

The sound of a revving engine captured his attention, and he swung his gaze around to the long stretch of road. Headlights appeared and he stepped in front of Gina, his adrenaline once again shooting skyward. There weren't supposed to be any cars on this road. Could it be the guys handling the roadblock?

No, they would have radioed ahead.

Mac stopped his trek back toward his truck and turned to stare at the approaching vehicle. When it passed under a street lamp, Ian caught a glimpse of something hanging out the window.

"Gun!" he yelled.

Heart pounding, he pulled his weapon and grabbed Gina's arm to propel her toward the cover of a van parked in the next-door parking lot.

She let out a scream and stumbled with him, slamming her body up against the vehicle just in time. A rat-a-tat sounded, bullets pinging left and right. Ian saw Mac dive for cover. A member of the CSU team hauled himself the rest of the way inside the car he'd been processing. Everyone else hit the ground.

Gun ready, Ian swung around the side of the van as the vehicle roared past. He pulled the trigger as fast as his finger would move.

More bullets sprayed the air around him in retaliation and he ducked, covering Gina with his body. His mind registered the thudding of the bullets hitting the van.

Grabbing her hand, he yanked her to her feet and shot his

former CO a look. The man's face had become granite, his G36 palmed and aimed, ready to do more damage. Mac looked over at Ian, and Ian signaled he'd be in touch.

Then he pulled Gina after him.

"How far can you run?" he shouted at her.

"As far as I have to."

TEN

Gina ran like the wind. One shoe flew off, but there was no time to stop and get it. Ian kept up a good pace and she stayed right with him, ignoring the occasional rock that bit into her tender flesh. She didn't want to think about what she might possibly step on. That didn't scare her nearly as much as the guys with guns.

Dodging cars and trash bins and the occasional late-night pedestrian, she flew along the sidewalk. Ian had dropped his grip on her hand, but she could hear him pounding behind her.

"Where am I going?" she shouted over her shoulder after they'd already run quite a way.

"Head to the hotel about half a mile ahead."

Half a mile. She could do that.

She saw the sign and energy surged within her. Hair whipping around her face, she aimed for the hotel. A sharp pain suddenly sliced her foot and she stumbled, would have gone down had Ian not reached out and grabbed her arm. He stopped, looked down, then swept her up into his arms.

She squawked, "What are you doing?"

"You're bleeding." His words sounded normal. He wasn't even winded after their crazy run.

And he had no trouble holding her securely against him.

"Bleeding?" Startled, she tried to see her foot, but he held her firm. "I am?"

"You must have stepped on a piece of glass back there. Come on, let's get inside and get that taken care of. What happened to your shoe?"

"I guess they were a little big. I lost it back there somewhere."

Shouldering his way into the hotel, he set her in the nearest chair and approached the desk. "I need a room, please." He fished out a fistful of cash and handed it over to the clerk. The thin man, who looked barely out of middle school, took the money and gave Ian a key.

Ian looked at Gina. He must have noticed her flustered expression because he said, "We're not staying the night, just long enough to get your foot cleaned up and some *more* necessary items delivered. Let me make a quick call and we'll take care of your foot."

"Okay." Several areas on her fatigued body throbbed with pain: her knee, an elbow and the bottom of her foot.

He got on the phone and she grimaced as she shifted on the vinyl-covered chair. The adrenaline high that she'd been on ebbed and her lids drooped. In spite of the danger she knew lurked behind the corner, she thought she might fall asleep right in that chair.

So she distracted herself by watching Ian pace and talk. Again, another surge of unexpected attraction for this man thudded her heart and caused her to blink.

She remembered the feeling of being carried in Ian's muscular arms. The man was huge compared with Mario, who'd been wiry and strong in his own right, but Ian's build dwarfed both of them. And he made her feel safe.

Even though she knew the men who were after her were

still out there, just having Ian close by dissipated some of her terror.

Some.

"All right, let's go." He stooped and scooped. Flinging her arms around his neck, she found herself face-to-face, practically lip-to-lip, with this extremely intriguing man. Uncertainty flooded through her as he stared down at her and she offered him a trembling smile.

He blinked, then turned on his heel to head down the hall to the room. He talked as he carried her. "I think we'll be okay here for a short period of time. We're not too far from where the shooting occurred, so there are cops everywhere, which will cause whoever's after us to think twice about hanging around. Mac will cover for us and take care of the legal stuff at the scene while we figure out how to keep you safe."

She watched his lips move as he talked. He'd almost kissed her back there in the lobby—she was sure of it. Butterflies attacked her stomach and she shivered. What had he been talking about? Her fatigued brain had just about reached capacity today.

He pulled her closer and said, "You're freezing."

Gina didn't bother to tell him he'd misinterpreted her shudder and that she was more than warm.

"Here's the room." Slowly, he lowered her to the floor, where she stood on her uninjured foot.

"Did I leave a trail of blood behind?"

"No, I was watching for that. The wound must be clotted, but you still need to clean it out." He pulled the key out of his shirt pocket and inserted it. The door swung in.

"Great." She sighed. Not exactly how she pictured her night playing out.

"Sorry."

And she could see sympathy shining in his eyes. He reached out to pick her up once more, but she held out a hand to stop him. "I can walk."

"Does your foot hurt?"

"Well, yes."

"Then no need." Once again, he scooped. She sputtered, then relaxed. Amusement danced in his suddenly unguarded eyes and Gina sucked in a breath. Wow.

"You're enjoying this, aren't you?" she asked.

A chuckle escaped him. "Kinda." Then he turned serious. "I'm not manhandling you, I promise. I just want to make sure there's not anything like glass embedded in there. You don't want to walk on it and shove it in deeper."

"Good point."

Carrying her just inside the room, he pushed the door shut with a foot. Then he set her on the edge of the bed while reaching behind him to pull up the desk chair.

"Let me see."

Without a word, she acquiesced.

Tenderly, he held her foot as he examined the wound. "I'm going to have to clean this up. Hang on."

Walking over to the sink, he grabbed a washcloth and soaked it in warm water. She watched him wring the cloth out and thought how comfortable he appeared. Mario always seemed to be moving, and when he did, it was with such energy and flamboyance that being with him for extended periods of time tended to exhaust her.

And yet, she'd loved him.

Ian returned with the washcloth and began cleaning. She flinched at the sting but didn't pull away.

"I know this hurts, but you don't want it to get infected."

Through gritted teeth, she said, "I'm fine."

He glanced up at her. "Uh-huh. It's actually not that bad. You should be able to walk on it."

"Like I said, I'm fine. How much time do we have before we need to get out of here?"

"Probably a couple of hours. I'll call Mac when I'm done with your foot and see where they are. I'll also have Jase deliver us another car."

"Tell him to make it a bulletproof one," she muttered.

A hint of humor flashed in his eyes. "Right. Keep up the good attitude—you're going to need it. We might be on the run for a couple of weeks."

"Couple of weeks!" She sat straight up, wincing as the pain in her foot bit at her.

Unfazed by her outburst, he simply looked up and said, "Yep. Now hold still. There's a piece of glass in there, I think."

She flopped back and sighed—then yelped and sat straight up. "Hey!"

He held up a small sliver of glass and said, "Now you should start feeling better. When was your last tetanus shot?"

"Two years ago when I sliced my hand on a rusty nail."

"Good. That's one thing we don't have to worry about. When Jase gets here, he'll have a first-aid kit on him. I'll bandage it up and we'll be good to go."

"I hope you told him to bring me a pair of sneakers."

Jase brought the car. Ian gave it a thorough examination finding it to be clean of any tracking devices. One more lightning-fast stop found Gina a pair of comfortable shoes that fit, since Jase had neglected to bring that necessary item.

Then they were on their way back up the road, retracing

their steps. Ian drove past the area they'd just run from a couple of hours earlier. The roadblocks had been removed, as had most of the evidence that there'd been a shooting.

"The car's gone."

Ian nodded. "They took it back to the lab. Mac texted me. They found a tracking device on the inside of the hubcap. That's how they found us so fast. He also said that two of the officers who set up the roadblock are dead."

Gina gasped and felt tears fill her eyes. "Oh, no. I'm so sorry."

His hand covered hers. "It's not your fault, Gina."

"But…"

"But nothing. It's not your fault."

She drew in a ragged breath and whispered a prayer for the men's families. *Oh, Lord, what have I gotten myself into? What has Mario gotten me into?*

Blinking back tears of grief for two men she didn't know, she blew out a sigh. Determination hardened her jaw. "All right, now we have even more reason to find out what's going on and who's involved. Where to now?"

"Back to the beach house? We need to see if we can find some financial papers or statements. Anything that will tell us which banks to start with. And we need to match that key up to a safe-deposit box. I really think that's going to tell us a lot."

She thought about that for a brief second, then shook her head. "No. He wouldn't have that kind of stuff there. That house was his haven, his escape from the real world. Financial records and stuff? That equaled work." She shot Ian a glance. "I guess we need to go back to where all this started. With me, in Spartanburg."

Without hesitation, Ian made his way to the exit that

would lead them away from the beach and west toward Spartanburg.

Weariness clawed at her, and she leaned her head back against the seat. A warm hand covered hers, and she opened her eyes to see Ian looking at her. The expression on his face did strange things to her stomach, things that Mario's looks had never elicited. Guilt overtook her.

With what she hoped was a subtle move, she shifted, withdrawing her hand from his.

His eyes shuttered, and he focused on the dark road before them. So much for subtlety.

He said, "Why don't you try to get some sleep? It's about a four-hour drive. I'll wake you when we get there."

"Where's there?"

"Good question." He lifted a brow at her. "Your parents?"

"No way. I don't want to lead these guys to them."

"You're right about that. How about Joseph?"

She paused, thinking about it, then nodded. "I guess it's going to have to be him."

"Joseph is FBI and Catelyn is a homicide detective with the force. I agree that might be the best place to stay."

She paused and looked at him. "How did you know about Catelyn?"

He blinked. "I did my homework when you called. I never go into a mission without a thorough briefing."

"All right. Give me your phone and I'll see if that's okay with them."

Ian handed over his phone and Gina punched in the number. Joseph answered on the second ring. "Hello?"

"Hi, Joseph, it's me."

"Gina, are you all right?" Joseph's burst of words nearly deafened her, and she pulled the phone from her ear. He

emanded, "What's going on? Any progress on the case? Is
an with you?"

"We're on the way back to Spartanburg. Yes, some prog-
ess. Yes, Ian is with me. Now hush."

"Sorry."

"I really don't want to go back to my house—yet. Could
we stay with you?"

Without hesitation, he said, "Absolutely, I'll tell Catelyn
to expect you. She's working a case right now on the other
side of town, but we've got plenty of room. You know that—
you sold us the house. Ian can use the small efficiency apartment across the drive, and you can have the guest room."

Relief flooded her. She hadn't realized how stressed she'd
been about the thought of returning to her home. Although
she knew she'd have to face it soon, she also knew it
wouldn't be pretty.

"Thanks, Joseph. See you soon."

She handed the phone back to Ian. He slipped it into the
cup holder. "Go ahead," he told her. "Get some rest."

"What about you?"

"I'll get some when I know you're safe and we've found
who's after you."

She stilled, reading the concern in his eyes, the determination to get to the bottom of all of this. An unexpected lump
formed in her throat. Why was his leaving the unit consid-
ered so awful? What had Ian done to enrage Mario so? How
could she believe that he'd done something to betray them?

She couldn't.

And yet, the facts were there. He'd left at a critical time.
They'd just finished a successful mission. Morale was high,
emotion flowing. And he'd asked to be reassigned. Why?

But she wouldn't ask him again.

And he wasn't volunteering the information. So why d
Mario trust him, tell her to go to Ian when she was
trouble? There must be some reason. A strong reason.

Hammers started pounding on her temples and she sh
her eyes. *Lord, I don't know what to do. I don't know why*
of this has happened, and I don't know what was going
with Mario and what it is I'm supposed to have. I guess
don't know much of anything. Please, God, get us safe
through this…and help me figure out these feelings I seem
be developing for this man beside me. Is it okay, God, to ha
these feelings? Is it right? And how do I ignore them unti
find out why Ian left the unit? Or do I even need to know?

Her prayer seemed to loop over itself with a string
endless questions. Finally, her prayers faded, her muscle
relaxed and she drifted.

With a start, she jerked awake and looked at the clock
Eight-thirty in the morning. She'd been asleep for three an
a half hours.

And during that time, no one had shot at them or tried t
run them off the road. Amazing.

She looked at Ian. He sat straight, almost rigid, eyes o
the road, the only sign of his own weariness in the groove
beside his mouth and a few extra wrinkles around his eyes
Other than that, he looked as if he could keep going fo
several more days. That was a Ranger for you. A thought hi
her. "Did you check on Nicholas? Is he all right?"

"I talked to him a little while ago. He has a little hideawa
not on the house blueprints. He's fine."

Relief flooded her. Then she looked at him. "Are you okay?

He glanced her way. "Yeah, I'm all right. How abou
you? Feel better?"

"Yes, thanks."

"We've got about another thirty minutes. Then I need you to give me directions to Joseph's house."

"Okay. So, tomorrow..." She paused and frowned. "What's today anyway?"

"Thursday."

She gasped and sat up straight. " It's Thanksgiving Day?"

Ian barked a short laugh. "Yeah, I guess it is."

"I don't think I should try to see my family today. I don't want to lead whoever is after me to them. What about you and your family? What will they be doing? I'm making you miss Thanksgiving. I'm so sorry."

Ian shrugged and gave another laugh. "Relax, Gina. It's really not that big a deal. Carly will probably go home. Mom and Dad are used to not hearing from me and not being there for holidays. They won't even try to call."

"Ian, that's awful." She was appalled.

His lips twitched. "It does sound rather pitiful when I say it like that, doesn't it?" He blew out a resigned sigh. "But it's okay. This is my job, what I chose to do. Really—" he paused "—I suppose it's become my life."

"Why?"

He didn't answer and for a moment wondered if he would. Then he said, "I don't know. There's so much injustice in this world. So much hate. So many who are power hungry and greedy...." He shook his head. "It's wrong and shouldn't be that way, so each time we're successful on a mission, the feelings I get are...indescribable. I can almost call it a drugless high."

"Mario was like that."

"Yeah, I remember. Most of us are. We all have our reasons for choosing this profession."

"Mario's childhood had a lot to do with his career choice."

"He never said much about it to me, just that it was rough."

"His mother was involved in some pretty nasty stuff—drugs, prostitution, that kind of thing. By the time he was eleven, he'd seen more in his life than anyone, adult or child should see. Thank God child-protection services finally stepped in and sent him and his sister to live with his grand mother."

Ian shook his head. "I never knew all that. He never said a word about his past, but he had a raging passion to get the bad guys off the streets—no matter what it took."

"Probably because of his mother. He could hardly stand to talk about her. Blamed her drug addiction and inability to care for them on the crooks who sold the stuff."

"He loved the undercover assignments the most."

She smiled a little. "Yeah, he did." Then she sighed and looked at the ceiling. "What went wrong?" she whispered. "Where did he go wrong? What did he take that would make someone willing to kill indiscriminately to get it back?"

ELEVEN

Ian gripped Gina's fingers as he wheeled into Joseph and Catelyn's paved driveway. "I don't know, Gina, but we'll figure it out."

The door opened and Catelyn—in full detective uniform, gun and all—stepped out. "Gina! I'm so glad to see you." She rushed forward to throw her arms around Gina, who gladly gave the woman a tight squeeze.

"Hey, Catelyn, thanks so much for letting us stay here. This is Ian Masterson. Ian, my sister-in-law, Catelyn Santino."

The two exchanged greetings; then Gina asked Catelyn, "Where's Joseph?"

"He's tying up the loose ends of a case, but he promised me he'd call your mother and explain why we won't be there today."

"We? What?" Gina's eyes went wide. "No, no way. We're not ruining your Thanksgiving. This is Stefano's first, and I know Ethan and Marianna want to show him off." Marianna, Gina's sister, had married Ethan O'Hara, the detective who'd been in charge of finding the killer of Marianna's roommate a year and a half ago. Marianna had given birth three weeks ago to a son, her parents' first grandchild. Gina had popped in at the hospital to see the little guy; then a week later she'd walked in on the goons tearing her house apart.

Catelyn offered a little laugh. "We've been by to see that kid a dozen times since he was born. I promise, your mom and dad will be glad for two less people around to hog his attention. There's no way we're letting you spend Thanksgiving alone. Plus, we want to help you figure out what's going on and we can't do that in a room full of people." She turned serious. "Now, come on in and let's get you guys settled."

"Did we pull you from a case?" Ian asked as he stepped inside the house.

"Well, you know there's always a case. But nothing that won't wait an hour or two—and it is Thanksgiving. I'll get Gina settled in the guest room." She pointed Ian in the direction of the kitchen. "Ian, why don't you take the apartment across the drive? It's kind of like a mother-in-law suite. Just go back out the way you came in. You'll be able to figure it out."

"Thanks." He grabbed up his backpack and disappeared.

Catelyn turned to Gina and pulled her in the direction of the guest room. "Now spill it. What's going on?"

And so for the next twenty minutes, Gina filled her in on the details of what her life had been for the past two weeks. And how Ian fit into the picture.

"So, you trust him? With your life? After the fuss Mario pitched about the guy leaving?" Catelyn's skeptical expression said a lot.

"Mario sent me to him. Him, Catelyn. Not you, not Joseph. Ian. That says a lot to me. And I don't know why he asked for a transfer. He hasn't shared that with me, but obviously it's not anything that's going to put me in danger. Rather, he's saved my life a couple of times already." She shrugged. "I don't know what to think, to be honest with you."

Catelyn stood from where she'd been sitting and paced. "I only met Mario a couple of times. He was intense, a loner. But he was crazy about you. I'm having a hard time believing he'd do anything to put you in danger."

Gina pulled the letter from her pocket and handed it to her sister-in-law. Catelyn read it and gave a low whistle. "Wow."

"Yeah. A key was in my locket. So now I just have to figure out which bank he might have used. We called yesterday, but they were already closed. Even if they'd been open, we couldn't have gotten there on time."

"And no one is open today."

"Right."

A door shut and Gina jumped.

Had the people after them found them already?

Catelyn whirled, placing a hand on her weapon as she slipped out of the room and down the hall. Gina, heart in her throat, followed silently behind her.

They met Ian coming out of the kitchen, gun pointed in the direction of the sound they'd all heard. He must have come back in the house just as the door shut. Catelyn and Ian made eye contact, and Catelyn drew her weapon, moving with quiet stealth to the den area, then through to the back. Ian coordinated his movements to support Catelyn's. Gina bit her lip and tried to stay as silent as she could. Her eyes darted around the area, looking for a potential weapon.

"Hey, Catie? Gina? Where are you guys?"

Ian halted, Catelyn breathed in deep and Gina wilted against the nearest wall, the tension falling from her. "Joseph!"

Her brother rounded the corner and Gina threw herself into his arms. He held her close for a moment, then pushed her away. Spying Ian, Catelyn and the guns, he raised a brow. "Guess I should have called first."

Catelyn nodded. "Might have been a good idea. What are you doing here?"

"I got things settled a little earlier than I thought I would and wanted to check on my baby sister here."

Gina gave him another hug and then introduced the two men. Joseph studied Ian carefully. Ian held his gaze steady and let the man come to his own conclusions.

Finally Joseph gave a small smile and held out a hand. "So you're the one. Good to meet you."

"Thanks." Ian shook his hand.

"All right, guys, what's the plan?" Gina asked as her pulse returned to normal.

The four of them walked into the den and settled onto the comfortable furniture to discuss what they needed to do next.

Ian spoke up. "Joseph, is there any way you can help us find out who to contact at First Spartanburg and Palmetto National banks? I know it's Thanksgiving, but…" He shrugged. "I just feel like we can't sit around eating turkey while someone out there is after Gina."

Her brother nodded. "I agree. I've got some pull around here. Let me see what I can find out."

He left the room and Catelyn turned to Gina and Ian. "You two are exhausted. Why don't you go grab a couple of hours of rest while Joseph works on this? I'm sure he'll let you know as soon as he figures something out. And I'll be on the lookout for anything hinky." She patted the weapon at her side.

Gina stood and ran a hand through her hair. "I'll take you up on that. I had a few hours sleep in the car, but I don't know the last time Ian slept."

He waved aside her concern. "I'm fine."

Catelyn gave him a stern look. "You're not fine. Even Rangers have to rest at some point. Go." She pointed toward the kitchen, the direction of the detached apartment.

Ian flushed and ducked his head. "Yes, ma'am."

Gina knew he gave in so easily because he knew Catelyn was right. Even he had to have some sleep eventually. And now was the time to do it, with an FBI agent and a homicide detective in the house as protection.

He made his way from the den to the porch door that led outside. "Wake me if Joseph finds out something."

Gina nodded. "We will." Ian finally exited the house. She turned to Catelyn. "Are Mom and Dad terribly worried?"

"Pretty anxious, but Joseph's reassured them that you're all right, you're just mixed up in a legal issue that needs to be solved."

"Good. Has he got someone watching them? To make sure they're all right, I mean?"

"Yeah, they don't know it, but they're under a 24/7 guard."

A weight fell from her shoulders. The thought of something happening to her family made her stomach clench.

Catelyn took Gina by the shoulders and steered her toward the bedrooms. "Go, rest while you can."

"Right." Gina gave her one more hug and said, "Thank you so much for doing this."

"I'd have been mad if you hadn't asked."

Ian awakened with a start, heart pounding, sweat running down his face. He'd been dreaming. He laid back with a grunt. All was quiet, the studio apartment still and cozy warm. Too warm. Getting up, he padded across the room to open the window. It cracked slightly and cool air rushed in.

He noticed the bars on the outside of the glass and wondered who had felt the need for such protection. Which brought him back to Gina. Protection and his responsibility for keeping her safe.

He let himself begin to process all that had happened. He thought about the man he'd seen in the hallway at Nicholas's house. Decked out in army fatigues carrying all the right hardware.

A Ranger. No doubt about it. Or if he wasn't a Ranger, he'd been supplied with all the right Ranger equipment.

So, Mario had been right. There was a traitor in the unit. Maybe more than one. Although, one question that surfaced was whether the traitor was actually from Mario's unit—or a different one? There was no way to tell at this point. The only thing they could do was watch their steps and cover their backs.

One thing was for sure: only someone with highly developed skills such as a Ranger—or some other branch of special ops—could have breached Nicholas's security. The person would've had to have been able to get his hands on a set of blueprints of the house, acquiring not only the layout but also the alarm-system plans.

Only the attackers hadn't counted on Nicholas's justified paranoia. As a judge he received death threats on a regular basis. With a nephew and niece to protect, he'd personally installed his own secondary silent alarm. That was the alarm that had alerted them to the presence of last night's intruders.

While Gina slept in the car, Ian had called Nicholas to check in. He'd learned that as soon as the attackers realized their prey had escaped, they'd left the premises as quietly as they'd approached. The authorities had tried to follow but were quickly left behind.

Nicholas was unharmed, having hidden in his private haven behind his house—something else that was not on the blueprints.

So, where did that leave him and Gina?

Who had betrayed them? How did they know where to find them?

Jase?

Mac?

He hadn't told either of these men where he was going. His cell phone was encrypted, virtually untraceable.

So, how?

His mind clicked through the possibilities.

And landed on the only possible explanation.

The computer he'd used at Nicholas's to access the decoding software.

The breath rushed out of him.

So, someone was tracking his movements, too, someone who had his information at his fingertips. Someone who knew he might access that kind of software. He hadn't been tracked from Nicholas's end; he'd been tracked through a secure software he'd used on numerous occasions.

This was not good.

A knock on his door had him pulling the gun from under his pillow and rolling to face the possible threat. However, he realized if the person on the other side of the door wanted to harm him, he probably wouldn't have knocked.

"Who is it?"

"Joseph. I've got something for you."

Ian shoved the gun back under his pillow. "Come on in."

Joseph opened the door and stepped inside the small studio house. He had a tray of food and a thermos of coffee. Ian felt his mouth start to water and gratefully took the burden from Joseph's hands. "What'd you find out?"

Joseph took a seat in the desk chair and leaned forward, elbows on his knees. "I called the bank managers and had them go in and look up the information for me."

Ian grimaced as he took a sip of coffee. "Bet they loved that."

Joseph shrugged. "I told them a woman's life was on the line and they were pretty willing to help out."

"And?"

"And Mario did bank there, but he didn't have a safe-deposit box at either one."

Ian frowned. "That's odd."

"Then the only thing left to do is to go to my place and let me go through Mario's things."

Both men turned at the sound of Gina's voice. She stood there, looking small and vulnerable, her dark curls unbound and wild about her head.

Ian swallowed hard, nearly choking on the coffee he'd just drunk. Dressed in baggy jeans with fashionable holes and a pink, long-sleeved T-shirt, she was beautiful.

She was also barefoot.

"Don't you ever wear shoes?" he blurted.

One dark brow reached up to disappear underneath a black curl. "Not if I don't have to."

"How's your foot?" he asked, referring to the place she'd cut during their mad dash from their attackers.

She wiggled her toes. "Fine. Sore but fine."

Joseph's gaze ping-ponged back and forth between the two, and when Ian finally turned his attention back to Gina's brother, speculation gleamed in the man's eyes. Ian just smiled.

"Well?" she asked.

Ian blinked. "Well what?"

"Are we going to my house to see if we can find something in Mario's things about a safe-deposit box?"

"Yeah. Let's do that."

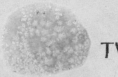

TWELVE

Ten minutes later, they were in the car and on the way across town to Gina's duplex. Located on the ground floor, it shared a wall with the house next door. There were two units per building.

Ian pulled into her parking spot as per her directions and shut off the car. "Stay here while I check it out, okay?"

"You think someone might be watching?"

"I don't know. I didn't see anyone on the way over here. I circled the block twice, but that doesn't mean someone isn't keeping an eye out in case you come back."

Gina shivered. "Great." She handed him the key and stayed in the car while he went inside. The fact that he simply pushed the door open instead of using the key didn't bode well for what she was going to find inside. She'd left so fast two weeks ago she hadn't even called the police, although the crime-scene tape across her door indicated her neighbor or someone else had. No wonder Joseph had been so worried. The police had no doubt contacted her family to ask if they'd seen her.

Guilt stabbed her. She should have called them sooner than she had.

Ian waved to her from the door. She could come in.

The grave look on his face added to the dread already churning in her gut. She got out of the car and met him on the small front porch. "How bad is it?"

"Pretty bad."

"Irreparable?"

"No, probably not. Do you rent or own it?"

"Own. I'm a Realtor, remember? Renting is like a sin," she teased, although there was no lightness in the act and the smile slid off her face almost before it had a chance to form.

"Right. Then the police probably did their thing and left. No landlord to worry about. Although, I would have thought they'd have locked the door behind them."

Gina slapped a hand against her mouth and muttered around her fingers. "My poor family."

"Joseph took care of all that, right?"

"Yes, he just sounded so frantic when I called him from Nicholas's house."

"Of course he was crazy with panic. You're his baby sister. If it had been Carly…" He didn't bother to finish and merely shook his head.

Anger at Mario shot through her and she fisted her fingers. "Boy, I wish Mario was alive so I could give him a piece of my mind." Then guilt hit her and she bit her lip. "Of course, if he were alive, we wouldn't be in this predicament."

Sympathy coated Ian's features. "Are you ready to come in?"

She scuffed a toe against the sidewalk and looked up at him. "I guess I've delayed it long enough, huh?"

"Yeah. Sorry, it's pretty ugly."

Squaring her shoulders, she took a deep breath and stepped inside. Ian placed a hand on her lower back and guided her forward. The first shiver that zipped up her spine had nothing

to do with the destruction before her and everything to do
with the man beside her. The second one shook her entire
being. Pictures had been slammed to the floor. Tables, chairs,
lamps were overturned. Couch cushions slashed, the insides
leaving a trail of white stuffing all over the floor.

"I can see now why Joseph was so frantic," she muttered.
"When he saw this, he must have freaked."

"Freaking is putting it mildly," a voice behind her said.

Gina whirled to see her brother standing in the doorway.
He sauntered in, his relaxed posture a direct contrast to the
rage simmering in his eyes. "Thought I'd see if you guys
needed any help." He waved a hand toward the devastation.
"I was going to call in someone to come clean it all up, but
the police didn't want to release the scene quite yet. They
were still working on some stuff and thought they might
come back here. And I didn't want to mess anything up if
there was a clue to your whereabouts."

His didn't say the words outright, but she could see he'd
been terribly worried about her. "Thanks, Joseph. I'm going
to be fine as soon as we catch whoever's after us. And I'm
really sorry I didn't call sooner."

"I know." Hands in his pockets, he came farther in and
shot a glance at Ian. "Anyway, after you left the house, I got
to thinking you might need some backup."

"Catelyn sent you." Gina gave him a small smile.

One side of his mouth tipped up in a half smile. "Yeah,
but I was thinking it anyway. Even though I'd already
informed the captain you were all right, I called him on the
way over here, and he said since you'd turned up, he
wouldn't hold the scene anymore. You can do whatever you
need to now. So—" he rubbed his hands together because it
was chilly in her place "—what's first?"

"My laptop. Maybe Mario left something on there. He knew my password."

Ian's lips slid into a wry grin. "If he wanted to put something on your laptop, he wouldn't need your password."

Gina gave a self-conscious laugh. "I guess not."

With the guys on her heels, she walked into her bedroom—and gave a shriek when she saw the devastation. Black fingerprint dust coated every surface. Her pillows had been slashed, drawers pulled out and thrown across the room. Her vanity mirror was shattered...and her poor laptop—it lay broken in two pieces: the screen was on her bed and the bottom part that held the keyboard clung precariously to the edge of her nightstand.

Stuffing down her growing anger, she grabbed the keyboard, flipped it over and looked at the bottom. "They took the hard drive."

Ian sighed and ran a hand through his hair. "You know, that's just stupid. It took some work to get that hard drive out of there. Why wouldn't they just take the whole thing? Why risk being caught?"

Joseph's eyes narrowed. "I don't like this."

Gina paced. "You think it means something?"

"Yeah." Ian nodded, mouth tight in a grim line. "I think it means they did all this destruction as a message. It's overkill, unnecessary."

"So, what's the message?"

He gestured to the gaping hole in the keyboard where her hard drive had once been. "They want you terrified. So scared you can't think straight."

"I'd say they're on the road to success there," she muttered.

"This stuff is too deliberate." He walked over to her chest

of drawers and leaned down to pick up an empty picture frame with shattered glass. "What was in here?"

She gasped and felt the color drain from her face as she bolted to his side to snatch it from his hands as though she needed to confirm the frame was empty. Joseph grabbed her elbow. "What is it, Gina?"

"Why would they steal a picture of me holding Marianna and Ethan's baby? It was from the day he was born. We were all at the hospital and taking turns holding him." She looked up at Joseph. "You took that picture."

Ian and Joseph exchanged a glance, and Joseph immediately pulled his phone from his pocket. Nausea made her weak, the fear spinning through her veins set off uncontrollable trembles. "They'd hurt a baby?" she whispered.

Ian closed his eyes and shook his head before answering. "Yes, unfortunately, they would—if they thought it would advance their cause or force you into helping them find what they're looking for." He caught her before she fell. "Come on."

Leading her back into the den, he lowered her to the couch, doing his best to soothe her fear. "Sit here and catch your breath. Joseph's on the phone with Ethan right now. They'll have an entire police force of protection surrounding them. They'll be fine."

She appreciated his efforts, but the words bounced off her brain; they couldn't seem to soak in. *Please, dear Lord, protect them.* Gathering her strength took everything she had in her, but she straightened her spine and comforted herself with the knowledge that Ian was right. Ethan had a whole slew of friends who would watch out for baby Stefano and Marianna. Now it was up to her to help stop whoever was making these threats against her family—and trying to kill her. "We have to find them, Ian. We have to keep them from…" She stopped and drew in a deep breath. "Mario's stuff. Let's go through it and see what we find."

His eyes sharpened. "You don't think the people that searched this place found it?"

She shrugged and stood on shaky knees that were only slightly more steady than when she realized that picture was missing and what it might mean. "I don't know, but I wouldn't think so. I have everything packed away in a chest that's outside in my storm cellar."

Hope brightened his eyes. "Storm cellar?"

"Sure, it came with the place. Come on. The key is in here. At least it was." She pushed open the door leading into her kitchen—and gasped as she took in the sight of more destruction. Her refrigerator had been pulled away from the wall and thrown to the floor. It lay on its side, door open, its meager contents strewn about. This, on top of the computer, stopped her cold. More nausea churned within her for a moment and she just stood there, staring at the appliance, getting herself under control once again.

Warm hands settled on her shoulders and pulled her around into a gentle hug. "You can do this, Gina. You're safe and your family is safe."

"They wrecked my home," was all she could think to say. And it wasn't the material things she was so shattered about— it was the invasion of privacy, the stripping away of her security. It was her escape from the world…. Or it had been.

"We'll put it back together. You'll see. We'll do a little cleaning, a little dusting." He paused. "Some new furniture and a nice Christmas tree right there in the corner by the window. It'll be perfect again."

"Ian's right," Joseph said, stepping into the room. "I wanted to clean up the mess, but, like I said, didn't want to go messing with anything until the scene was cleared. Fortunately, you didn't have much in there to spoil so the place doesn't stink. If you guys want to head down to the cellar, I'll start cleaning this up."

Gina pulled her head from the comfort of Ian's chest, turned and searched the dark eyes that looked just like hers. "Did you warn Ethan?"

"I did. He's taking care of things on his end. Let's take care of things on ours."

Ian gave her one last squeeze, and Joseph's speculative gaze made her blush. She pulled away from Ian's arms. Arms she could get used to having around her. Grateful for his support, she took strength from the fact that she wasn't in this alone. Moving to the last drawer on the right-hand side of her dishwasher, she opened it.

It looked untouched. Had her untimely arrival interrupted the search before they'd gotten to it? Probably.

Gina reached in and pulled out the key to the cellar and led the way outside. It smelled like snow, but she wouldn't hold her breath. It rarely snowed in this area, although it did get very cold. She shivered as she made her way over to the edge of the fence that lined her small backyard.

"It doesn't look disturbed."

"They probably didn't even think to look out here," Ian murmured. "I wouldn't have."

She leaned down and inserted the key into the lock. It opened easily, and Ian pulled open the door for her.

A damp, musty smell greeted her, and she wrinkled her nose as she flipped the light switch at the top of the stairs. A single bulb illuminated the area as she started down.

At the bottom she took in a deep breath. "Okay, there's the trunk right over there." She pointed to a far corner and made her way over to it. "It was his grandmother's cedar chest." Memories assaulted her, and she stopped to pull in a fortifying breath.

Ian asked, "Do you want me to open it?"

"No," she murmured, "I'll do it. I just haven't looked in there since I packed it up." Six months ago, she'd lovingly placed each and every item into the trunk, saying goodbye to Mario with a finality that stabbed her heart like a knife. The worst part of his death, other than creating a hole in her life, was that she didn't know where he was. Heaven or hell? The uncertainty nagged her spirit, bringing a deep sadness to the depths of her soul whenever she thought about it. Not that she hadn't talked to him about faith and her love for the Lord. She'd tried her best not to be preachy or pushy but to lovingly guide him back to the God his grandmother had raised him to know.

She knelt before the chest and opened it.

Everything lay untouched, a lifetime reduced to a few items in a box. Pushing morbid thoughts away, Gina reached in and started pulling things out. Mario's favorite shirt. The CD he loved to listen to in his car. A picture of the two of them sitting on the beach, taken by a man who'd been out for an early morning jog.

And the hard drive that she'd forgotten about. It rolled to the floor with a thump.

"What's that?" Ian asked as he knelt beside her.

"Mario's old hard drive. He told me to bury it should anything ever happen to him. I was in such a hurry to pack up his house on the base that I just tossed it in here and forgot about it."

Ian took it from her fingers. "Mac brought me a laptop, but not the stuff I need to access this."

"Do you think there's something on here?"

"Who knows? We'll definitely need to check. But I need the right equipment. I could call Mac, but I think Jase might be the best one to contact about this."

"What kind of equipment do you need?" Joseph asked from the top of the cellar stairs.

Ian looked up. "Stuff to read this hard drive."

"I can get it for you. Let me make a call."

"Great."

Joseph turned to head back to the house and Ian stood. "Come on." He offered her a hand and she took it. He pulled her up and said, "I'm starving. Let's get a bite to eat while we wait for Joseph's contact to bring up whatever we need."

They returned to the kitchen, and Gina saw that Joseph had accomplished quite a bit in cleaning up. Her refrigerator stood back where it belonged, although the dent in the side didn't bode well for future use. Four large trash bags, filled and tied off, sat ready for the dump. Not bad, all in all. Having the room look halfway decent slid a measure of peace back into her soul.

They found Joseph in the den, straightening furniture and trashing broken items. He looked up when they came in and said, "I called Catelyn and she called the department's computer forensics guy. He's going to bring some equipment over to my house. Catelyn also threw together some lunch stuff. We can eat and work at the same time."

Gina raised a brow at her brother's efficiency. "You got someone to come over on Thanksgiving Day?"

"He owes Catelyn big time. She proved his nephew innocent of a hit-and-run charge about a year ago."

Ian looked around. "All right. We've probably spent too

much time here anyway. Let's take separate routes back to your house just in case anyone's watching."

Joseph nodded. "Good idea. I'll meet you there."

Her gaze bouncing between the two men, she felt a lump form in her throat. *Thank you, God, for the protection you're providing. Please continue to keep us safe.*

Ten minutes later, Frank had his computer set up and the hard drive rigged to go through that system. Ian hovered over the man's shoulder, watching. Gina stood next to him, leaning into him a bit. His heart thumped at her nearness. How he wanted this thing finished, Gina safe and the possibility of pursuing a relationship with her a reality.

"Well, that's interesting," Frank said.

"What?" Gina pushed in closer, trying to see the screen. Ian moved aside for her so she could.

"The hard drive's been wiped clean except for a few files."

"What kind of files?"

The man shoved his nose closer and clicked the mouse a few more times. A bank statement appeared. "Probably the ones you're looking for."

"What's the name of the bank?" Ian asked.

"Sparkle City National."

Gina crossed her arms over her stomach and blew out a breath. "I didn't know he used that one. He never mentioned it."

Frank shifted to look up at them. "Do you want to print this stuff off?"

"Not yet. Keep looking. What else do you have?"

Frank went to the next file and said, "Hey, it's a receipt."

"For?"

"A safe-deposit box. It was scanned and saved as a picture document."

"What's the date on it?"

Frank zoomed in to the corner that held all the information. "Um…just a little over six months ago."

Gina leaned in closer, and Ian placed a hand on the small of her back. "Three days before he died," she whispered.

Ian looked down at her. "He wanted you to find this.

Mario's leading us on a merry chase, but at least he's making the clues easy to find."

She shook her head. "I don't understand why he couldn't have just told me everything in the letter."

Ian rubbed her shoulder. "He was doing his best to keep you safe. If the bad guys had gotten their hands on you, all of this…craziness…would have bought you time. Time enough to get help, escape, whatever."

She bit her lip and looked away. Joseph's keen eyes took in the interaction between Ian and Gina, and Ian knew her brother might have a few words to say before this was all over and done with.

Gina straightened her shoulders and tossed back her silky curls. They landed on his hand, and it was all Ian could do to resist sliding his fingers through them. He dropped his hand. Once again, it wasn't the time or the place.

He said, "Okay, so we know we need to go to Sparkle City National. It's closed today, but first thing in the morning, we need to be on their doorstep when they open."

Gina nodded and touched the locket resting at the base of her throat. "I've got the key. Let's see what Mario was willing to die for."

Gina turned over and looked at the clock. As tired as she was, she couldn't sleep, and now it was 2:00 in the morning. After Frank had been sworn to secrecy and left, Ian and Gina had brought Joseph and Catelyn up-to-date on everything.

Before she knew it, she'd fallen asleep on the couch to the sounds of Joseph and Ian hammering out a plan. She'd awakened around 1:00 a.m. to find someone had covered her with a blanket and turned all the lights off.

Grumbling at the crick in her neck, she'd scrambled off

the couch and made her way to the guest bedroom, where she'd fallen onto the bed.

Wide-awake.

An hour ago.

With her mind clicking at warp speed, trying to process everything up to this point. What were they going to do? Would tomorrow's visit to the bank answer all their questions or just stack more questions on top of the already-towering pile?

Sighing at her inability to fall back to sleep, she sat up and flung the covers from her. Padding over to the desk, she flipped on the lamp, blinking at the sudden brightness.

Why couldn't she sleep?

Because there was simply too much going on. Too many unanswered questions to let her mind shut down. She must have felt safe enough with Ian, Joseph and Catelyn right there in the room with her to allow her to fall into such a sound sleep. Now...

Something flickered in the dresser mirror.

What?

Fear darted through her and she flipped the lamp off. There it was again. The mirror sat exactly opposite the large window. Gina had pulled the curtains shut when she'd walked in the room, not able to bear the thought of someone being able to see in. Yet they were white sheers. Light passing over them would easily penetrate the thin fabric. But she was facing the back of the house, not the street side, so why was there light outside her window?

Had whoever was after her already found her? Shuddering at the thought that she might have placed Joseph and Catelyn in danger, she crept toward the window, stood to the side and gently pushed a bit of the curtain aside so she could look out.

Horror hit her as she took in the sight of the separate apartment across the drive—where Ian was staying.

Flames and smoke rolled from an open window. The only window that wasn't covered with bars, preventing any kind of escape.

Ian coughed and drenched himself in the shower, clothes and all. In swift, efficient movements, he wrapped sopping towels around his hands and head, then flung one over his shoulders.

The sound of shattering glass had jerked him from a restless sleep. The only reason he'd actually been able to fall asleep was the fact that Gina had such good protection inside the house across the drive.

A foot-long gas pipe had exploded when it hit the floor and rolled under the bed. Fortunately, he'd fallen asleep on the couch on the opposite wall. Otherwise he'd be dead instead of singed. Thank God there hadn't been any shrapnel or other sharp objects in the pipe, or the bomb would have caused a lot more damage. His cell phone, now fried to a crisp, had been in the middle of the bed, tossed there while Ian had showered. He'd left it there as he'd settled on the couch to study the files on Mario, wondering if he'd missed anything the first fifty times he'd looked them over.

Smoke and flames quickly filled the small efficiency apartment. Heat seared him as he'd raced for the door—only to find it barricaded shut from the outside. No amount of ramming it with his shoulder had worked, and the knob refused to turn.

So he'd soaked himself in the shower as best he could to enable him a little more time to find a way out.

The bars across the window offered no escape. The bathroom window was too tiny to wedge himself through. His best hope was to protect himself, find a way to get out the door and pray someone from the house had awakened to see what was going on.

Gina called 911, reported the fire, then ran down the hall yelling for Joseph.

"Joseph! The apartment's on fire! Get up! Get up! We've got to help Ian! Jos—"

Catelyn appeared in the doorway, tying the knot of her robe. "What is it?"

Then Joseph stepped around his wife looking rumpled but wide-awake, pulling a shirt on as he headed for the back door. "Stay inside! We don't know who's out there."

Joseph yanked the door open and Gina watched him run across the drive to the burning apartment. Ignoring his order, she chased after him. Catelyn grabbed her gun and was quick on Gina's heels.

"Ian!" Gina screamed. "Ian!"

The smoke scorched her lungs but she didn't care, didn't stop. She had to get him out of there. Had to do something to help him. The thought of losing him nearly buckled her knees. She kept going until she could go no farther.

Sirens sounded in the distance.

Joseph disappeared into the small attached garage that housed Ian's car. Catelyn stepped up beside Gina and curved an arm around her shoulders. "You're a target, Gina. You shouldn't be out here. Why don't you go back inside?"

Gina shrugged her off. Her heart pounded with fear and dread. "No, not until I know Ian and Joseph are okay." She coughed and narrowed her eyes against the smoke.

Once again, Catelyn protested and Gina snapped, 'What would you do if that were Joseph trapped in a burning building?"

The fact that the woman stood there as Joseph ran into the flames was answer enough. And while worry stamped itself on Catelyn's pretty features, she didn't say anything more as she reached over to grasp Gina's hand in hers.

Grateful, Gina squeezed her sister-in-law's fingers and prayed.

Fervently.

Ian thought his lungs were going to explode. Wet rags could only do so much against the smoke. He had to get out and get out now.

Studying the door, he latched onto an idea that might work. Pulling his knife from the pack he'd grabbed from the side of the bed before his mad dash to find the door barricaded shut, he opened it to the largest blade and went after the hinges on the door. The top one popped off with no trouble

The second one came out with a bit of a struggle. Sweat ran down his face. His whole body felt as though he were on fire, but he had no time to worry about that. And no time to go for the third hinge as dizziness consumed him. He jammed the largest blade of the knife between the door and the frame and pulled. The blade snapped.

Ian growled in frustration, then coughed until his head ached. He went back to the door, using another blade from the knife, but it was hopeless. The hinges didn't want to separate. This was an old building, built in the late 1800s, and this door was most likely the original, made of solid wood and tight hinges.

And if he didn't get it down, he was going to fry.

"Ian! You in there?"

Joseph.

"Yeah!" Ian coughed. "Kick it in!"

"It's been barricaded. Stand back!"

From his position by the wall, he heard a lot of banging that seemed to go on forever but in reality was only a few seconds. Someone probably had used a long two-by-four and some duct tape. Quick, simple, efficient and—if he didn't get out of here—deadly.

Then a well-placed kicked rocked the door. Another one did the trick. The hinges let go of each other and the door fell in. Ian glanced at the door and felt only grim satisfaction at his correct assumption. A two-by-four had been fastened horizontally from one side of the door frame to the other. The duct tape clung to the doorknob.

With no time to dwell on the fact that someone had just tried to kill him, Ian hurled himself from the flaming apartment into the garage. Joseph grabbed his arm and led him into the cold night air.

Immediately they were swarmed by firefighters and paramedics. Water pelted his face—and a small body with strong arms wrapped herself around him even as he coughed the smoke from his lungs.

He hugged her back; then she was gone and he had an oxygen mask slapped over face.

A paramedic ordered, "Lie down on the gurney, sir, and let us check you out."

Ian waved them away. He had to keep an eye on Gina. This could have just been some huge diversion to get at her. "I'm fine," he rasped and winced at the burn in his throat. But he did suck in one more breath of oxygen. Only to lean over and cough spasmodically once again.

Joseph caught his arm. "Gina's okay. Catelyn's with her. You need to get checked out."

"No way. We need to get Gina out of here. This fire could be a diversion."

"They didn't come after Gina. They came after you."

Ian stilled at this, coughed once more and realized Joseph was right. "Unless they thought she was staying there."

Joseph was shaking his head even before Ian finished his thought. "Negative. She never went near that apartment. They were watching. They knew who they were after tonight. You."

FOURTEEN

Gina palmed away the tears from her sooty cheeks. Ian was all right. She paced the kitchen floor, desperate to see him. She'd been shoved aside as the professionals snatched him from her to check him over. Catelyn had insisted that Gina stay in the house out of sight, and now that Gina knew Ian was all right, she could do that.

He was safe. *Thank you, Jesus.*

She kept repeating her thankful three-word prayer until she heard the door slam, then felt herself pulled against a strong chest. "I'm all right," he whispered in her ear.

She nodded, the lump in her throat blocking the words she wanted to say. "Did you talk to the police?"

"Just enough to keep them from asking more questions. I referred them to Mac. He'll keep them out of the equation."

"Thank you," she whispered.

"All right, there's nothing more we can do tonight. Tomorrow—er, today—we'll head to the bank. Depending on what we find there, we'll decide what to do next. Deal?"

She looked up at him. He still had his arms around her and they felt so right. Ignoring the sudden thumping of her heart, she nodded. "Deal."

He kissed her forehead and said, "Go sleep. Catelyn will wake you in time to get ready."

"What if they come back?"

Joseph stepped into the house just in time to hear her question. He shut the door behind him. "I've called in some reinforcements. Something I obviously should have done earlier this evening. However, I've redeemed a couple of favors and will have two guys watching the house the rest of the night. It's a temporary solution, but at least we can all get some rest."

Ian gave her one last squeeze, produced another violent cough, then said, "I'll grab the couch. And I need to call Jase to get me another cell phone."

Catelyn protested, "We can make room." She shot a glance at Joseph. "I told you we should have bought the three-bedroom ranch-style across town."

Joseph just shook his head.

Ian spoke up. "I'd rather stay here. If they make it past your guys and through the door, they'll have to go through me." He pulled his gun from the pack he'd managed to grab on the way out of the burning apartment. He shoved it under the couch pillow that would cradle his head as soon as he could lay it down.

Joseph and Catelyn exchanged a look; then Joseph said, "Fine."

At the knock on the door, three hands reached simultaneously for weapons. Joseph walked to the door and peeked out the window. He then waved to the others that everything was fine and put his gun away. Opening the door, he stepped outside.

When he came back in, he carried an oxygen tank and mask. "Here," he said to Ian, "since you're so stubborn and refused to go to the hospital, one of the paramedics brought this for you. He said to use this tonight and to please return it tomorrow. I'll be bunking on the other couch, so I can keep an eye on you tonight."

The large den boasted two oversize couches that formed an L shape, one along each of the two walls. Catelyn had insisted on enough seating for Joseph's huge family.

A grateful look crossed Ian's face as he consented to the oxygen. Gina knew he was having a hard time breathing. Each rasping breath that he took in whistled in his lungs. When she'd had her head against his chest, she could hear the wheezing. Then he frowned as he registered the last part of Joseph's comments. "I'll be fine. You can sleep in your own bed."

Gina rolled her eyes at Ian's protest.

"Ian, give it up," she said. "Quit being so stubborn and accept the help you've got."

He gave one more weak attempt at insisting Joseph would be more comfortable in his own room, then finally gave up when he realized he couldn't win against the three of them. Catelyn got the necessary linens and while the guys went to shower, Ian in the full bath off the hall and Joseph in the master bath, Gina helped her make up the two couches.

Gina placed a hand on the woman's arm. "I'm sorry about all this, Catelyn. I don't know how they knew we were here."

Catelyn gave her a brief hug. "Don't worry about it. It's surprisingly easy to find someone when you have certain resources at your disposal. And the apartment out there was just a building. A nicely insured, easy-to-replace building. You're what's important, you and Ian. Your safety is the priority, you got it?"

Tears threatened for the umpteenth time that night, but Gina managed to hold them back and nod. "Thank you."

A freshly showered Joseph entered the room and headed

for the door. "I'm going to check with our bodyguards. Be right back."

Ian came in about a minute later, coughing, but she thought he sounded a little better. She gestured to the oxygen tank. "You're going to use that, right?"

He quirked a grin at her. "Yeah, I will. I promise."

Catelyn said good-night and headed back to bed. Gina lingered, exhausted beyond belief; however, she wasn't quite ready to let this man out of her sight—a fact that startled her and made her question once again his reason for leaving the unit. She was sure it wasn't anything illegal or immoral. When he'd first left and Mario had been so tight-lipped and angry, she'd wondered.

He sat on the couch, a thoughtful expression on his features. She sat beside him. "What are you thinking?"

Ian blinked in surprise as Gina tentatively reached out and took his hand. Then his heart warmed and he squeezed her fingers. "You're not ready for sleep?"

She shrugged. "I don't sleep very well these days."

"That's understandable."

Small talk. He could do that. Just being in the same room with her seemed to make everything a little better.

He wrapped an arm around her shoulders, gave her a slight squeeze, then said, "We're going to catch these guys, Gina."

She smiled up at him. "Thanks for saying *we*."

"Not a problem." Her innocence and sweetness seared his heart. How he wanted to protect her, find the people responsible for the dark shadows under her eyes and weary droop to her shoulders.

Another cough racked him and he wiped the tears that still leaked from his bloodshot eyes. Gina wrapped both of her hands around one of his and whispered, "I'm sorry I'm so much trouble."

Ian took a deep breath after the spasms eased and gave a little laugh. "You're no trouble. The guys after you are the ones that are trouble."

"I know, but I just feel so bad that…"

"Drop it," he ordered gently. "I'm not going anywhere until we get these guys." He flexed a shoulder that had been slightly singed. "They have to be stopped and apparently think I'm a threat to whatever they're up to, since they came after me. That's a good thing."

"What? How can you say that?"

"Because if they weren't worried, they wouldn't have tried to kill me. And they got a bit careless tonight."

She frowned at him. "What do you mean?"

"That pipe bomb they sent through my window was made in a hurry, a spur-of-the-moment kind of deal."

"What makes you say that? How do you know?"

"Because it didn't have any little pieces of glass, nails or shrapnel in it. They used what they had…gunpowder."

Gina shuddered. "So what does that mean?"

"It means they must be getting a bit desperate, grabbing at opportunities instead of carefully planning an attack."

Worried, she chewed her lip. Ian reached up to pull it from the snare of her top teeth. "Don't do that. It's going to be all right."

Butterflies took flight, diving in her belly and then fluttering all around. "I…know."

"Do you really?"

She studied him carefully. "I think I do."

His gaze dropped to her lips and his head lowered a fraction. Gina didn't move. Didn't dare to hardly breathe.

The door opened and Joseph came in, rubbing his hands against the chill of the night. Ian drew back and allowed a small smile to cross his lips before turning his attention to Joseph.

Joseph's brow raised at the sight of Ian and Gina sitting so close together on the couch, and his eyes seemed to spark in amusement; then that disappeared as he said, "The police finished questioning the neighbors." He tossed a small package to Ian, who caught it. "Your buddy had this delivered."

Ian straightened from his relaxed position on the couch, coughed and winced as he asked, "Anyone have anything useful to say?" He opened the package and pulled out a cell phone.

Jase, efficient and speedy, had come through for him.

Joseph was saying, "Not really. Mr. Johanassen said he was up, going to the restroom, when he heard tires squealing. When he looked out the window, he saw the taillights of what he thinks was a truck disappear down the street."

Ian blew out a sigh. "You're right. Not much help there."

"Everyone seemed to wake up after the fact."

Gina stood. "It's very late. We only have a few hours until we need to leave. I'll go on to bed and let you guys try to get some rest."

Joseph stepped forward to pull her close for a tight hug. "We'll see you in the morning, sis. Get some sleep."

Gina entered her room and looked at her rumpled bed. Sleep. Right. *Oh, Lord, please protect us.*

Eventually the sun popped up over the horizon, and Gina watched it happen. She'd managed to doze off for a couple more hours, but by 6:00 a.m., she knew it was hopeless to lie there any longer.

She got up, showered and got ready to go, having

borrowed a clean set of clothes from Catelyn. And all the while the locket hung around her neck like an albatross. Yet, she cherished the item because of whom it had belonged to.

Mario's grandmother had been such a special lady, filling a void in Gina's life that had been left when her own grandmother had passed away a couple of years ago. Gina liked to think she, too, brightened the old woman's life just a bit; losing her only granddaughter had been a crushing blow to her, and Gina's arrival seemed to put a light back in her eyes.

Gina fingered the piece of jewelry. It was the only item that had come home with Mario's sister's body after she'd been killed in the cross fire.

The knock on her door startled her. "Come in."

Catelyn poked her head in. "Just thought I'd check on you. I made some French toast if you're interested."

"I'm interested, thanks."

"Ian's already up and champing at the bit."

Gina allowed her lips to curve. "Does he think they're going to lct us in early?"

"Joseph got the bank manager's number and pulled him out of bed. He's going to let you guys in as soon as you get there."

Gina followed Catelyn out the bedroom, down the hall and into the kitchen. Ian shot to his feet. "Are you ready?"

"Sure." She grabbed a piece of toast from the table and a bottle of water from the fridge. "Let's go."

What should have been a ten-minute drive to the bank turned into a thirty-minute scenic route as Ian kept a careful watch behind him. He still coughed occasionally but seemed much better than when she'd said good-night to him last night.

"Are you okay this morning?"

"I'll live."

Yes, he would. No thanks to her. She bit her lip, wondering if…

"I'm not leaving you, Gina. It's not your fault all this is happening."

She jumped. "So you're a mind reader now?"

"No, but it doesn't take a genius to interpret what those little lines of worry are between your eyes, or the way you chew on your lip. And from the discussion we had last night, I thought you might be thinking along those lines."

Gina blew out a sigh and sat up a little straighter as the bank building came into view. "You're right—I was. But right now it doesn't matter. We're here."

"Yep. I'm just going to circle the block a couple of times."

Wilting back into her seat, she ordered herself to be patient. Yes, she wanted to know what was in the safe-deposit box, but she wanted to be alive to see it, too.

Two more laps around, Ian finally pulled into a parking spot and cut off the engine. A black Honda sat in the spot in front of them. He said, "Joseph said to look for that car. It belongs to Stan Holcombe, the bank manager. We're going in the back way."

Gina looked at her watch: 7:16 a.m. They should have the place to themselves for a while. Climbing out of the car, they approached the back door. A security guard opened it and allowed them entry. "Mr. Holcombe is waiting for you. He asked me to come in a little early."

Gina felt sure that Joseph had warned the man to take some extra security precautions until she and Ian left the bank.

Stepping inside the warm area, they followed the guard through a series of short halls, arriving at a tastefully decorated office. Stan Holcombe sat at his computer but immediately stood when he saw his visitors. A tall man in his early sixties, he exuded competence and a genuinely friendly smile that instantly put Gina at ease. Clear green eyes twinkled down at her as they exchanged introductions.

She asked him, "Did you know Mario?"

"No, ma'am, I can't say I had the pleasure. Now, if you'll just show me some form of identification and sign this admission form, we'll get started."

Gina signed the paper, then pulled her license from her purse and handed it over to him.

He picked up a paper from his desk and compared the two signatures. "Gina Santino. Excellent. If you'll follow me, I'll take you right to the safe-deposit box and you can conduct your business."

"Thank you." They followed the man down another hallway and came to the room. Anticipation jumped inside Gina as Mr. Holcombe headed for the door that would allow access to whatever it was Mario had deemed important enough to hide in a bank. Yet, she felt confused, too. She'd never signed the papers to rent the box, so why was her name listed as a renter? And even more weird, why did the signatures match?

Chilled, even though the room was warm, she rubbed her arms.

Oh, Mario...

As soon as the banker was out of sight, she turned to Ian. "Mario must have forged my name on those papers."

Lips tight, he nodded. "That's what I figured, too, when I realized your name was on them."'

"I can't believe he did that…. He forged my name and actually got away with it!"

"He was a Ranger, Gina. You'd be surprised with what we can get away with." He didn't sound particularly proud of that, more like he was simply stating a fact.

"So he opened it three days before he died. That means he acted as soon as he realized he was in trouble—and that he needed to find a way to protect you."

She shuddered. Sympathy flashed across his face and he pulled her to him in a spontaneous hug. Grateful, she leaned into his strength, taking comfort in his presence.

Then Mr. Holcombe was back, setting the box onto the table in front of them. "You have your key?"

"Of course." Gina fumbled for the locket. Once again, Ian helped her remove it. The banker said nothing as Ian pulled the key from its hiding place, his placid demeanor implying he'd seen it all. One more weird couple in his bank was nothing to raise his brows over. Instead, he pulled the guard key from his pocket and motioned for Gina to go first.

Taking the key from Ian, she placed it in the designated slot and twisted it. Faintly she heard the tumblers inside release. The banker then inserted his and did the same.

The box was unlocked.

FIFTEEN

After Stan Holcombe left the room, Ian looked at Gina. She stood staring at the box as though it contained a poisonous snake. "Are you all right?"

"I'm scared to open it. Just like the chest in my cellar— I guess I want to know so bad and yet...I don't."

"Do you want me to?"

She hauled in a deep breath and reached out to touch the box. "No, I guess not. Now or never, huh?"

With shaking fingers she lifted the lid.

And stared.

Ian looked over her shoulder. A single sheet of drawing paper, about twelve by eighteen in size and covered in strange markings, was the only thing in the box.

With shaking fingers, she reached in and pulled it out. It had been folded a number of times, then stretched out flat on the bottom of the box. "That's it?"

"It means something," he reassured her. "Mario wouldn't have put it in there if it didn't."

"But how am I supposed to figure it out?" She pulled out a chair and slumped into it, still staring at the paper. With a growl of frustration, she slapped it on the table. "Why did he have to make this so difficult? What's the point?"

Ian slipped into the chair beside her and took her hand. The tears shimmering in her bottomless dark eyes rocked him. She wasn't used to this kind of thing. Her nice, orderly life had been shaken to the core. For him, this was business as usual—if one didn't count the fact that the woman he loved was in danger and he didn't seem to be getting any closer to catching the guys who wanted to hurt her. "It's going to be all right, Gina. And the only point I can think of is that Mario thought it best. He was taking extra measures to protect you."

She swiped her eyes. "I know, I know. Sorry. Guess I just needed to whine a moment."

Ian brought her hand up and kissed her knuckles. "You're entitled."

Face flushed, she pulled her hand from his and gave a jittery laugh. "Well, let me look at this for a bit."

Mentally, Ian gave himself a kick. What'd he go and do that for? He watched her and decided she didn't seem to mind too much. Encouraged, he scooted a little closer to see the paper even as he examined his heart.

Yes, he still loved Gina. Now more than ever.

Did he feel guilty that he was picturing a future together with Gina once all this was over? Assuming they made it through alive?

Yes, he did.

He moved his chair back a bit. *Sorry, Mario.*

And yet, Mario was dead. He'd loved Gina. Surely he wouldn't want her to mourn him forever. Would he?

Not the Mario Ian had once known, but it looked like Ian hadn't known the man as well as he'd thought.

His phone rang.

Mac.

He looked at Gina, who'd raised her head at the sound. He said, "I'll just be over here. Go ahead and keep doing what you're doing."

She nodded and Ian headed to the other side of the room, clicking open his phone. "What do you have for me, Mac?"

"Mario was undercover. I've figured that out. Only he was undercover on his own. I don't know what he was working on. All the unit guys are being tight-lipped but are admitting that Mario was being a rogue, going off on his own."

"Great." Ian sighed and looked at the ceiling. *Mario, how could you be so stupid?*

Or was it stupidity? Ian had a feeling Mario had acted the way he had because he felt as though he didn't have a choice. Because he didn't trust his guys.

Mac said, "His grandmother left him a tidy sum of money and that farm out in the country, but as far as I know he never set foot there once she died."

"Huh."

"And, uh…"

"What?"

"I've got some pictures."

"Of?" Cold dread curled in Ian's belly. Somehow he knew he wasn't going to like this.

"Mario and some chick. We're looking into it, trying to figure out who she is."

"Where did the pictures come from?"

A pause. Ian clutched the phone a little tighter. "Mac?"

"Jase gave them to me."

The cold dread turned to a sick hollow feeling. Jase? *Those* pictures? The ones Mario had threatened to kill him over? And for some reason Jase had given them to Mac. Interesting.

He cleared his throat. "All right. Thanks, Mac. Call me back if you find the identity of the woman in the pictures, will you?"

"Absolutely."

A gasp from the table caught his attention, and he turned to see Gina on her feet, working on the piece of paper from the box. "Gotta go, Mac."

He clicked off and walked over to Gina. "What are you doing?"

Excitement thrummed through her. "I think it's a puzzle."

"What do you mean?"

"Oh, you know Mario. He loved puzzles, codes—and origami." She folded one piece to match up two arrows. The seemingly random lines connected, forming one long one.

"Okay, what's next?" she muttered, almost to herself. "Which ones go together next?"

"Try these." He pointed to two arrows.

She folded, then gave him a look of approval. "Good job."

He shot a smile at her, one that glowed with warmth. The place on her knuckles where he'd pressed the briefest of kisses still tingled. She rubbed her palm against her jeans and focused on the paper.

"Here, let me try this one." She folded it. "That doesn't look right, does it?"

"No. I think all the lines are supposed to connect."

"Yeah, you're right. They are." She tried another one and felt a surge of satisfaction when the lines merged, this time to curve around the edge of the page. Another fold. "It's a picture!"

"A drawing," Ian agreed.

Gina looked at the clock. They'd been in the room for forty minutes. She started to sweat. Staying in one place too long caused her nerves to jump.

"What did Mac have to say?" He grimaced and she paused, pinning him with her gaze. "What?"

"Mario was definitely working on something on his own. Something he didn't want to share with the guys in the unit."

"We already knew that."

"Right, but apparently he was doing something deep undercover."

"But how is that possible? How could he do the job he was supposed to be doing and do something on his own? He couldn't be in two places at the same time."

Ian paced and motioned for her to keep working.

"He must have been called out of cover for something. Something serious enough to warrant blowing his cover."

She turned back to the paper, but her mind clicked through this new information. "That training session he was supposedly killed in... Is there any way to find out for sure how he really died?"

"I've asked Mac and he's sticking to the story."

She shook her head. "I just have a feeling it was something else. With all of this going on and the guys after me...I'm not buying the training exercise. If he was running for his life, setting up this crazy—" she waved a hand searching for the right words "—scavenger hunt," she finally blurted, "then what was he doing going back to participate in some training exercise?"

She folded another section of the paper.

Ian ran a hand through his hair. "I know. I've wondered that myself. And all this craziness was smart, believe it or not. He was making sure you stayed useful. Just in case you were caught by the guys who were after whatever he had. All of this stuff—" he gestured toward the paper "—it's all something only you could figure out. At least in a timely manner. If anyone else had been able to get into that box, they would have been stumped. But you…you've already figured it out."

She studied the paper again. "Yeah, I guess you're right."

Ian rubbed the back of his neck and said, "I can probably get my hands on the autopsy report." He looked at his pack, which held the laptop courtesy of Mac.

Gina shuddered. "Can you do that without jeopardizing anything? Like your job?"

"Don't worry about it. I'll make a few calls first before I use…alternative methods to gain information I need."

She raised a brow. "You mean 'Rangerish' methods?"

Ian gave a chuckle. "Right. Now, what have you got there?"

She looked down and made one more fold.

The picture was complete.

"It's a map," Ian offered.

"Yes. There aren't any buildings or anything. It's just the layout of some land." She pointed, saying, "See, here's a small lake or a pond. And over here, this looks like some kind of a barn or something. Then over here is a property line? But what prop—" She cut herself off with a gasp. "Wait a minute. I know where that is. That's the farm!"

"The farm?"

Excitement oozed through her. "The one Ian's grandmother willed to us." She gave him a spontaneous hug, then stepped back, not embarrassed one bit, just grateful he was by her side, walking with her through all this.

"Then that's where we go next, right?"

"Right."

SIXTEEN

The thirty-minute drive to the farm had Gina nibbling her nails and looking over her shoulder. Ian drove with a focused concentration, watching his tail while following her simple directions. His cough seemed better, so she was guessing he hadn't inhaled as much smoke from last night's fiasco as she'd feared.

"Do you have the key?" he asked as he turned onto the gravel drive.

She slapped a hand to her forehead. "No. I can't believe this. I didn't even think about the key."

He shot her an amused look. "It's all right. I don't really need one, but it does make things easier."

"Ha-ha. Cute."

Then all joking stopped as the house came into view. "Somebody's been taking care of this place. It looks exactly like it did the last time I saw it. Better than last time, actually."

"How long ago was that?"

"About a month after Mario's grandmother died. Toward the end she was pretty sick, and we had to come take her to the hospital." Gina stepped out of the car. "She never came home. Mario didn't want to touch the place for a long time, but I finally convinced him we needed to pack some stuff away and take care of…those things you take care of after someone dies."

"It was hard for him."

She nodded. "First, his mother willingly abandoned him to social services when he was eleven and Patrice, his sister, was just a year old. Mario told me she didn't even put up a fight when they came to take them. Then Patrice was killed by that monster in Colombia.…" She shook her head. "He was never really the same after that, I don't think. At least according to his grandmother's stories. I met him shortly after the fact."

"Yeah, he never talked about his sister, just that he'd like to get his hands on the guy that killed her."

"Unfortunately, he never had that chance." Gina stepped out of the car and walked toward the front door of the house. "I wonder who's been watching over this place."

"Mario probably hired someone."

"Sure, in the beginning, maybe, but he's been gone six months. I doubt he paid someone that far in advance."

"A friend of his grandmother's maybe?"

"Possibly."

She tried the door. Locked, of course.

"Here, let me help."

He stepped in front of her. She couldn't see what he was doing, but within about five seconds the door swung open. Chilled air greeted her and she shivered.

Ian entered and went straight to the stack of wood next to the fireplace. "This is a great house."

"I know. Mario loved it." She swallowed hard. "We were going to live here after we were married."

Ian nodded and turned his attention to getting a fire going. "Looks like someone's had a fire here recently." He held up a pack of matches and she frowned. Weird.

Gina flipped the switch on the wall. The overhead ceiling-fan light brightened the room. "Huh. The power's on, too."

"I gotta admit, it's kind of strange. I'm going to take a look at the thermostat. If the power's on, it shouldn't be this cold in here."

He wandered down the hall while Gina looked around, soaking in the memories the place evoked. She loved coming here and visiting, had planned her future around Mario and this home. Had pictured herself raising children here.

She blew out a breath and thought about Ian. He'd come to her rescue, no questions asked. What shocked her was the feeling that had erupted inside her. Being around Ian made her feel safe, secure and unsteady all at the same time. Deep down she knew he was an honorable man, one who put God first. And that drew her to him more than anything else. She was falling for him. Hard.

Ian walked back into the room and said, "Well, it was turned down pretty low. I inched it up, so between the fire and that, it should feel good in here pretty quick."

She just looked at him.

He blinked. "What?" Then narrowed his eyes. "What is it, Gina?"

It was her turn to blink. "Nothing. Sorry. It's this place… It brings back memories."

"Good ones, I hope." Skepticism played across his face as if he hadn't bought her simple explanation for her weird behavior, but he was letting her get away with it.

That brought a smile. "Yes, mostly good ones."

A scraping sound outside the door had them whirling toward it; then Ian had her by the upper arm and was pulling her down the hall and out of sight of the door. Finger to his ips, he gestured for her to be quiet. Eyes wide, fear raging once again, she nodded.

Another sound, this time resembling a thud. Something dropped? The sound of a key turning the dead bolt. Some of her terror dissipated. The guys after them wouldn't have a key to the front door.

Right?

She peeked around the corner. Ian stood to the side of the door, gun drawn. As the door opened slowly, he shifted, reached out his left hand, grabbed the knob…and yanked.

A hoarse yell greeted his efforts and a rifle skidded across the wooden floor to bump against the wall. Gina raced for it and snatched it up. Spinning, she took aim, only to stop and stare. Ian had his gun against the head of the intruder.

SEVENTEEN

Ian saw shock blanch Gina's features white. She yelled, "Ian, stop! It's Mr. Carswell."

He snapped the pistol up and away from the man's head. "Who are you?"

Bravado tried to overcome the fear on the weathered face without much success. "Jesse Carswell. I'm taking care of the place."

"Why?"

"Because Mr. Anthony paid me to do so."

Gina stepped forward. "When did he set that up?"

"A couple of months before his grandmother died. She was real sick and couldn't keep the place up. So he set up arrangements for me to come in and do it on a regular basis."

"And you've continued to do it without getting paid?"

The man gave a phlegmy chuckle. "No, I still get paid. Or I will through the end of the year. After that," he shrugged, "I don't know."

"You do know that Mario…um…died, don't you?"

He flinched. "Yeah, I'd heard that, but the money keeps getting deposited into my account each month, and I figured someone would be back one day to do something with the place, so…" Thin, bony shoulders lifted in another shrug.

"So you just kept honoring your bargain," Ian finished for him.

"Yup, that about sums it up."

Ian walked over and picked up the rifle from under the far window. "What are you doing with this?"

"Ya never know who—or what—you're going to run into these days. I saw your car out front and figured I might need to chase you off."

He reached for the weapon and Ian handed it over to him. Gina spoke up, "Thank you. I appreciate you taking care of everything around here."

"My pleasure, ma'am. It sure would be a shame to see this old place go to ruin."

She gave him a gentle hug. "It's good to see you again, but you don't have to worry about this place anymore. I'm here and I'll take care of it from now on."

Mr. Carswell nodded. "As it should be. I'll just get on back home, then."

"Tell Mrs. Carswell I said hello."

The man nodded and waved as he stepped back outside, making his way down the well-tended path. Ian sighed and shut the door only to turn and open it again. "Hey, Carswell."

The man spun around. "Yeah?"

"Have you seen anyone around here? Anyone who looked like they didn't really belong?"

He rubbed his stubbled chin. "Well, now that you mention it, there was a guy who came by asking some questions about this property."

Ian's eyes sharpened. "What kind of questions?"

"Oh, just how to get in touch with the owner, that kind of

thing. Said he was a Realtor and that his clients had driven by and decided they just had to have the place. I told him I didn't have a clue how to contact you."

Thank goodness for that.

"Did this guy give you a hard time about not knowing? You know, was he persistent?"

"At first he didn't seem to want to take no for an answer, but I finally convinced him I just didn't know."

"What happened then?"

"He left and ain't been back as far as I know."

"Can you describe him for me?"

"Well, let's see. He was big, like he worked out a lot. Dressed in a nice suit, he had dark hair and…and I think his eyes were blue."

"Did he have any tattoos? Earrings?"

Mr. Carswell scratched his balding head. "Yeah, seems like he had a tattoo on the back of his hand."

Suspicion leaped inside of Ian. "What kind of a tattoo? Did you see what it was?"

"I think it was some kind of dragon or…um…a reptile. Maybe a snake?"

"If I get a picture of him, do you think you could positively identify him?"

A shrug. "Probably."

Ian nodded. "Thanks." He pulled out a card. "Give me a call if you see him again, will you?"

"You got it. Take care." He pocketed the card, then disappeared over the far hill that led to his neighboring property. Ian turned back to find Gina studying the pictures on the mantel. She picked one up and traced the photo with a fingertip. "Patrice was Mario's pride and joy. He never got over her death, I don't think."

Ian looked over her shoulder, inhaling her spicy scent. "She was beautiful."

"Yeah, inside and out, from what I understand."

She replaced the picture and turned to look up at him. He cleared his throat and stepped back. "Mr. Carswell's story about a Realtor's clients picking this place to inquire about is just a little too coincidental to me."

Gina frowned. "Do you think it's one of the guys looking for us?"

He blew out a sigh. "I think so. I can't say for sure until I confirm a couple of things, but…I don't know. I need to—" he broke off "—I'm going to call the sheriff and see if he's noticed any strangers around town asking questions."

"If they knew I inherited the house, they may have come here looking for me. Finding the place empty, they would have gone into town. Is that what you think?"

He nodded, impressed at her ability to reason things through almost as quickly as he. "That's what I think."

Pulling out his phone, he called information to get the sheriff's nonemergency number. The operator put him through and the phone rang several times before it was picked up.

He identified himself and asked to speak with the sheriff.

"He's not in the office right now. I can patch you through to his cell."

"Thanks."

Once again the call was routed.

The sheriff answered on the second ring.

By the time Ian hung up, he felt as if he had a few answers. He made his way over to Gina, who had begun searching the room while he talked with the sheriff.

"Hey."

She turned, brow raised. "Yeah?"

"Is there a fax machine around here?"

"No. Mina wasn't very high-tech. Whenever Mario came to visit, he brought his laptop. Why?"

Conflicted about what he needed to do and what he wanted to do, he walked over to Gina and pulled his gun from his shoulder holster. "Here. Do you know how to use this?"

She looked up from the drawer she'd been searching through and took it from him. "Yes, Joseph taught all us girls how to use a gun when he finished going through the academy. Ian, what's going on? What did the sheriff tell you?"

"I'm going to have to ride into town. I called to ask if he'd had any strangers in town that really stood out. He did a little investigating for me and said his buddy who owns the diner remembered a man who'd come in asking a lot of questions yesterday. He said the guy was abrupt to the point of being rude when he didn't the answers he was looking for. The owner did a little search on his security videos and managed to come up with one of this guy. He'd sent it to the sheriff. I've got to go look at it."

"Oh, so that's why you wanted a fax machine."

"Yeah, so he could send me some still prints from the video. He could send them to my phone, but he said he didn't think they'd come through. They're kind of grainy."

"Can't someone drive it out here?"

He shook his head. "I asked." He stepped forward and cupped her chin. "I don't want to leave you, but you can't come with me."

Biting her lip, she nodded. "I know. I can't take a chance that someone I know—or who knows me—will see me and know I'm here. If they come back and start showing my picture around, I'm toast."

"Exactly." Using his thumb, he gently pried her bottom

p from her top teeth. He sucked in a deep breath and tepped back. "I'll bc as fast as I can. Joseph's on the way. Ie's about twenty minutes out."

She gripped the gun and made sure the safety was on. What if you need this?

"I can take care of myself." He leaned over and planted kiss on her forehead. "Let's figure this out and end it with s on the winning side."

"Sounds good to me."

Ian moved toward the door. "I'll be back shortly."

Ear tuned to any noises that might foretell of impending langer, Gina paced the spotless kitchen floor, wondering where she should search next.

Mario had sent her here. To the house that he knew she loved. She fingered the gun, praying she wouldn't have a need for it. The fact that Joseph was on the way offered her some comfort. She hated the thought of Ian having to fight off these very skilled…*assassins* was the word that came to mind, and she shivered in spite of the warming temperatures inside the house.

Closing her eyes, she tried to picture where Mario would have hidden something.

Nothing came to mind.

She'd have to do a methodical search through the house, possibly the barn. Starting in the kitchen, she went through every drawer, every nook and cranny. She even knocked on the wood and listened for a hollow sound, indicating Mario had gotten creative and designed a hiding place.

No luck.

The search did bring forth memory after memory, and she found herself alternating between smiling and tearing up.

Mina, Mario's grandmother, had been such a feisty woman—and a champion of the underdog. Which is why she'd taken in her two needy grandchildren at the age of sixty.

Gina moved into the next room, the den. Mr. Carswell had certainly earned his money. He'd done a fantastic job of keeping the place clean. Not a speck of dust anywhere.

Then an awful thought hit her.

Was it possible that Mr. Carswell could have found whatever it was these guys were after? Possibly unknowingly? Could he have found it and thrown it out? Was she searching for something that wasn't even there?

Sick dread curled in her stomach.

How would she ever know? It wasn't as if she could ask the man if he'd come across anything. She didn't even know what to ask *about.* A paper? A computer disc? A flash drive? A picture? Who knew?

Disheartened, she continued her search of the den—and came across Mina's Bible on the end table next to the oversize recliner.

How that woman had loved the Lord. Gina put it aside, promising herself she'd take the time to go through it later.

A few minutes later, she heard the crunch of a car on gravel. With her pulse speeding up a bit, she raced to the window and nudged the curtain aside a few centimeters.

Ian.

Relief made her knees weak. She hadn't realized she'd been so worried. Rushing to the door, she flung it open just as he stepped onto the porch. "Did you get the information you needed?"

"Yeah, I think so. I learned quite a bit."

She pulled him into the den. "I've been searching but so far nothing. You might as well fill me in on what you learned."

"I recognized a man on the tape."

She stilled. "Who?"

"Robbie Stillman."

"Who's that? A guy from the unit? I don't recognize his name."

"He was kicked out for dishonorable conduct about a month after he replaced me."

"And he's trying to kill me?"

"Looks that way. I thought that might be him when Mr. Carswell described the tattoo on his hand."

She slumped into the nearest chair. "So…Mario was right—there was a traitor in the unit."

"Well, he's not technically in the unit, but yeah, at least one traitor."

Lifting teary eyes to his, she said, "You think he was working with someone else?"

"Unfortunately, I do."

"Who?"

"I don't know. There wasn't anyone else in the video. Just Robbie. And he was definitely looking for you."

Her eyes went wide. "And?"

"He's been all over town, asking questions, causing quite a stir."

"Is he still here?"

"No, I never saw him. Apparently he cleared out sometime last night."

"To come burn down my brother's apartment?" she whispered.

"Maybe. My guess is he wasn't working alone, though."

"What makes you say that?"

"Just a gut feeling. The sheriff said another stranger had been in town, too, but he didn't have a picture of him. I bet they split up to ask questions. Robbie just happened to get caught on tape."

"Do you think he—they—know we're here?"

"Either they don't know we're here yet or they know and are forming a plan of attack."

"So, what do we do?"

"Be ready."

And keep searching. They had to stop running at some point, and Ian figured now was as good as any. Mario had led them to this house. They couldn't leave until they'd found whatever was valuable enough to kill for.

He had a feeling it was information on the guys chasing them but had no idea what kind or on whom. Gina pulled several books from the bookcase and started flipping through them, setting each one aside when she finished.

His phone rang. An unlisted number. Tensing, he flipped open the cell. "Masterson here."

"Hey, Ian, it's been a long time."

It took a moment for the voice to register. "Well, well, if it isn't Bandit McGuire. How'd you get this number?"

Gina stopped what she was doing and looked up at him. He waved her back to work and wandered into the kitchen. He wasn't sure he wanted her to hear his end of the conversation yet. She frowned at him but went back to work.

Bandit and Mario had been tight friends up until Bandit had seemed to disappear from the face of the earth. "Jase gave it to me. I heard you were looking into Mario's activities right before he died."

"Yeah, I am." Who'd told Bandit that? Why hadn't anyone mentioned talking to the man? Was he still deep undercover? Instead of voicing those questions, he asked, "Why? You ow something?" He was keeping in touch with someone he knew they were asking about Mario. With Jase? Mac? n didn't like the suspicions rearing their heads.

"Maybe. Jase saw Mario with some girl and snapped a w pictures of them together at some diner."

"Right. Mac told me about the pictures."

"Huh. Well, Jase found out who the girl was and passed at information on to me."

Anticipation curled through him, but he kept his deeanor calm. "Who was she?"

"Celestina Rodriguez."

A slug in his gut wouldn't have produced more shock. The daughter of…"

"Esteban Rodriguez. Yep."

"What was he doing with the daughter of the biggest unrunner in South America? Was he crazy?"

"Looks like it."

"Were they…romantically involved?" It made him sick o have to ask. Ian thought about Gina, innocent, unsuspecting, trusting.

"It sure looked like it, but if he was undercover, you never now what's real and what's not."

"Why did Jase take those pictures?"

Bandit blew out a sigh at this. "He thought Mario was cheating on Gina and took the pictures just to…aw you know, Jase, he was being a jerk."

"Huh. A jerk or was he just looking out for a good woman?"

The silence on the other end of the phone spoke volumes. Then Bandit cleared his throat and said, "Anyway, Mario was furious. Said he'd only seen her that once and threatened to kill Jase if he ever showed those pictures to anyone—especially Gina."

"Yeah, I know. Jase told me that, but he didn't know who the girl was."

"I know you and Jase were good friends once upon a time, but watch your back with him. He's trouble."

Sorrow gripped Ian. Had he trusted the wrong person? Could Jase have been responsible for Mario's death? Revenge for a threat? It seemed too far-fetched, but he'd heard of worse.

"What about Robbie Stillman? Have you heard anything from him in a while?"

"No, but I know he and Jase are pretty tight. They worked a mission together about a month ago."

"Jase and Robbie? Really?" Why hadn't Jase said anything about that? Doubts assaulted him from all sides. Who did he trust?

"Anything else?" Ian desperately wanted to pull out his laptop and do some research on the Rodriguez family but wasn't sure if it was safe. Whoever had tracked his movements from Nicholas's house might have hacked into the machine, allowing that person to know whenever Ian booted it back up. And if that person had that information, Ian and Gina's whereabouts could be compromised.

"That's it. You want me come give you some backup, man? From what Mac says, these dudes that are after you are dangerous. Why don't you tell me where you are and let me come out there and help?"

"Aren't you working something undercover? Where've you been all this time?"

"Yeah, I'm still undercover, but I can help out." He didn't offer any more information than that.

Who did he trust? *God, who do I trust?*

"Naw, I've got it under control. But I've got your number if I decide I need some help. Thanks, Bandit."

"Come on, Ian, you don't have to be the lone wolf here. o sense in going solo when you got help right here."

Ian paused. It would be nice to have backup he could unt on and yet…the whole story Bandit had just shared ith him just wasn't ringing true. Something was off. "I'll ll you if I need you."

He hung up. What held him back from accepting Bandit's fer of help? Suspicions tugged at him once more. That one call was just a little too convenient.

And if what Bandit said was true, what had Mario been oing with a gunrunner's daughter?

"Who was that?"

He spun to face Gina, who stood in the doorway to the itchen, chewing her bottom lip. "A friend of mine who eard we were looking into what Mario was up to right efore he died."

"And how did he know that?"

"From the guys in the unit Mac talked to, I'm sure."

Skepticism crossed her pretty face. "And you trust what e has to say?"

Ian hesitated. "I don't…mistrust it…. I just want to erify it."

"Right."

He glanced away, the urge to pull her into his arms and ury his face in her hair nearly overwhelming. He wanted o protect her, tell her everything was all right. Promise he'd et her out of this alive.

Instead, he swallowed hard and said, "I'm going to work on that. You keep searching, deal?"

Her eyes softened. "Deal, Ian. Thank you."

"Do you still think I betrayed the unit, Gina?"

The question popped from him before he could stop it.

Startled, she tilted her head and eyed him. "No. I don't guess I do. You must have had a good reason to do what you did Mario sent me running to you for help, so that says a lot."

"Maybe I'll be able to share my reasons for leaving with you one day." Soon, he hoped. But first he had to make sure she was safe. And would live to be a ripe old age, not cut down before she had a chance to experience love, marriage children.... He blinked and cut those thoughts off.

"I'd like that." She put her hands on his shoulders, stood on tiptoe and kissed his cheek. A blowtorch would have burned less.

Then she turned and left the room.

His phone rang and he snatched it up. Another number he didn't recognize. "Hello."

"Mr. Masterson?"

"Yes. Who's this?"

"Jesse Carswell. You asked me to call you back if I saw that man who said he was a Realtor."

"Right, right. And you've seen him?"

"Yup. He and another man just walked right past me and into the Rocking Porch Diner. They're flashing some badges and pictures and asking about you two."

EIGHTEEN

"Gina!"

She jumped at Ian's yell, dropping the vase she'd just turned upside down. Fortunately, it hit the cushion of the recliner and bounced. She caught it, settled it back in place and dashed toward the kitchen. Ian rounded the corner just as she did. He skidded to a halt, grabbed her upper arms and said, "Mr. Carswell called and said the guys were back in town. He recognized the car one of them was driving. Somehow I've got to figure out how to nab them and keep them from coming this way."

"But you can't confront them alone!"

"I'm not. I'm calling for backup."

"Who are you going to call? Who can you trust?"

"I've already put a call in to the sheriff and told him those guys are trouble. Joseph and Catelyn were almost here but are going straight to the diner instead." He cupped her cheek, studied her face a moment, then said, "I'm not going anywhere. There's no way I'm leaving you alone."

"No, you need to go."

"The sheriff's on the way. He's supposed to call as soon as he can."

"But...what if Joseph needs help?" The thought of her

brother and Catelyn facing down those men frightened her. Not that she didn't have confidence in Joseph's skills when it came to taking care of himself, but...

He cut his eyes toward her. "You trying to get rid of me?"

"No, I just can't stand to think of those men in town, around innocent people. People I may have put in danger because I came here." Tears filled her eyes and she blinked them away. "It's my fault. Maybe I should have just tried to disappear instead of trying to find whatever it is Mario hid."

"No. Now, you know as well as I do that would have been even more dangerous. If they're Rangers gone bad, they would have tracked you down. You played it smart and called me—so let me handle..."

His phone rang once more, cutting him off. "Joseph, did you find them?"

Gina resumed her search with a frantic panic. She had to find it. Whatever *it* was.

She moved into the bedroom and tore it apart. The house was so big. Four bedrooms and three bathrooms. Plus the basement and the barn. There was no time to search every spot.

Mario would have known this. Would have known she might be in a hurry and need to find whatever he hid. She closed her eyes and concentrated, picturing the letter he'd left her. She'd read it so many times she had it memorized. But nothing about it jumped out at her. Of course, the statement about "keep her close to your heart" hadn't made an impression the first one hundred times through either.

She headed for the office. She hadn't searched there because she figured it would be too obvious. Surely, he wouldn't hide something in his office. Then again...

Ian came up behind her. "They're not there."

"What happened?"

"They were already gone when Joseph and Catelyn arrived. They're searching for them right now."

"Do you think the guys after us are on their way here?" She felt tears of pure anger well up. Anger at Mario, anger at herself for her inability to figure out where he might have hid something, anger at the men chasing them. Just…anger.

"I don't know." Jaw tight, he reached back to rub the back of his neck. "All right, I'm not leaving you and there's nothing we can do about what's going on in town. The best thing we can do is search this place and find what we need to get these guys off our tail—and in jail. I'm going to search the barn. That'll cut some time off for you."

"Okay." She swiped the tears with her palms, and he reached out to brush a cheek with a knuckle. He looked as though he wanted to say something else.

Instead he said, "Keep your ears open. If you hear anything weird, get out of sight and punch in number one on your phone. I programmed it. Number one, then send and I'll know you need me, all right?"

She nodded. "All right."

"Then let's get busy."

Gina watched him leave, said a quick prayer, then got to work. Nothing in the desk drawers. Nothing in the filing cabinets.

She slammed one shut and wanted to scream. "Nothing. Where do I look, Mario? Help me out here, will you?" She ran her hands down her jeans. "I'm appealing to the wrong person, aren't I, God? I'm sorry. I just don't know where…" She stopped, looked at the picture on the wall and stepped closer. Wait a minute. The safe. It seemed that Mario had mentioned a safe once upon a time.

Behind a picture on the wall. But surely that was too obvious. There was no way he would have hidden anything there—would he? She pulled the picture away from the wall and stared at the combination dial in front of her. Without a doubt, she knew if Mario had put something for her in the safe, then the combination would be something she could figure out. Starting with her birth date, she worked her way through every number combination she could think of.

And stepped back with a groan. What would he use? Even his sister's birthday didn't work. Nor the day she died. Not even his grandmother's birthday.

With her head against her knees, she thought. Pictured every date, every number she could come up with. Lifting her head, she stared at the desk. At Mina's wedding picture sitting so innocently in its silver oval frame.

As though in slow motion, Gina reached for the dial once again and spun it to clear it out, then entered what should have been her wedding day.

The safe opened.

Gina reached in and pulled out stacks of papers, a picture album. Patrice's birth certificate—and death certificate. A stack of cash.

And a DVD player.

With a DVD taped to the bottom.

She had a feeling this is what she'd been looking for.

With shaky fingers, she reached for the cell phone to call Ian.

She turned the machine on and the home screen came up telling her to insert the disc.

Sucking in a deep breath, she followed the instructions, then pressed Play. Mario's face filled the screen and the breath left her in a painful whoosh.

"Hi, Gina," he said, "I guess you're still alive if you're watching this."

"Right. I'm still alive, Mario. No thanks to you," she muttered.

"I'm really sorry about the crazy chase I've led you on. And if you just stumbled on this by accident, don't worry about the chase I mentioned."

"What is it?" Ian asked as he stepped into the room.

She pressed the pause button and turned the computer so he could see it. "I found this DVD Mario made." She looked around. "In fact, he made it right here in this room. Have they found them yet?"

"No, not yet. They're still searching. I half-heartedly offered to come help, but Joseph threatened me with my life if I left you. I didn't argue."

"Here, watch." She pressed Play again as Ian scooted closer.

Mario spoke. "I guess I'm dead now. Let me just tell you that you can stop worrying about my eternal resting place. All of this has really brought home the fact that I need God. Everything you and my grandmother ever preached to me has sunk in. So, I'm good there."

Gina couldn't stop the tears of relief that flooded her eyes. Her heart ached with joy. *Thank you, Lord.* Ian's warm fingers curled around hers and squeezed.

"Anyway, listen, I guess you've figured out by now that I've got some pretty nasty people after me. Basically, it comes down to this—I messed up, big time."

"Who's after me, Mario?" Gina whispered to the screen.

"Our last two missions were in Colombia—where Patrice died." He swallowed hard and scrubbed his chin. "You'd asked me over and over what was wrong after I came home from that first one, but I just couldn't...share." His throat bobbed again and he looked straight at her. "I'm sorry for that. The authorities know it's the Rodriguez family behind her death. They just can't prove it. She was just in the wrong place at the wrong time. Five more minutes..." Tears welled in his eyes and Gina swiped her own.

"I started investigating her death and one day I saw Bandit McGuire. He signaled that he was undercover but wanted to talk. He'd catch up to me later."

Ian got up and checked the window, so Gina paused the video for a moment. "What's wrong?"

"I don't know. I feel like Joseph should have called me by now. They should have found those guys...or something."

"Why don't you call him?"

He gripped the phone so tight his knuckles turned white. Then he relaxed, walked back to her and said, "No, I'll give them a little longer. Let's finish seeing what Mario had to say."

Gina started the disc again. "That night, someone tried to kill me in my hotel room. Fortunately, I was the better fighter. I...uh...killed him and escaped to a bar up the street, where I called Mac. The television was playing. Time passed. Then suddenly there was a news flash saying Thomas Rodriguez had been found dead in a hotel room. Two days later, while everyone was at the funeral, I broke into the house."

Gina blinked. He'd broken into Esteban Rodriguez's home? "What were you thinking, Mario?"

How had he done it?

But he had skills ordinary men didn't have. And he'd managed something no ordinary person could have pulled off.

He spoke from the screen. "All I managed to find was a microchip stashed in a drawer. So, I snitched it, hoping something was on it, replaced everything the way it had been and left the way I came in."

He sucked in a deep breath and leaned forward. "This was the family responsible for paying the guerrillas who killed Patrice, and I'm going to get them, Gina. One way or another."

"You went after Patrice's killer. Oh, Mario, you should have told me." Gina shifted, narrowing her eyes at the screen.

"I knew the only way I was going to buy some time was to have some leverage."

Ian rubbed his face. "I have a bad feeling about what he's going to say next."

Mario stood, paced out of sight of the camera, then came back, sat down and cleared his throat. "I...uh...found Rodriguez's daughter, talked her into having coffee with me. I had this plan to...um...kidnap her and hold her until I could figure out what to do. Also for leverage when these guys came after me."

Ian groaned.

Gina closed her eyes and sucked in a breath.

"But it didn't work out. Jase—" Mario let out a disgusted humorless laugh "—the idiot, showed up. He...uh...took some pictures. Confronted me in front of Celestina Rodriguez and accused me of cheating on you. I said some things I shouldn't have and..." He rubbed his hands together, then scrubbed a hand through his hair. "Anyway, about that time, I noticed Bandit standing under the awning of a building trying to get my attention. He obviously didn't want Jase to know he was there, so I sent Jase on his way and met Bandit. An informant had come through and he needed someone to help him out, be a part of the team he already had there. I said sure.

"Only it's a setup. We get to the warehouse and Bandit

pulls a gun on me—tells me to give him the microchip." Now Mario looked embarrassed. He glanced away from the camera, then gave a rueful shake of his head. "I missed a camera." Then he shrugged. "I was in a hurry—what can I say? Bandit played the video for me, and it's clearly me stealing the chip from the office."

Gina groaned. "Why didn't you ask for help? And why was Thomas the one to go after you? Don't they have hired guns for that?"

She hadn't directed her question to Ian, but he answered anyway. "He was working with Bandit."

"What?"

"For some reason Bandit didn't want anyone to know he was still alive—or where he was living. On a chance encounter, Mario sees him. Bandit knows Mario will tell someone, so he has to get rid of him."

She closed her eyes. Had it all been a matter of being in the wrong place at the wrong time?

Mario continued. "Bandit admitted he's a part of the gunrunners. I knew he wasn't the leader, but he wouldn't give me a name. We fought—I shot him and escaped. Only now I'm wondering who else in the unit might be involved."

Ian stood and paced to the window. Gina jumped. She'd been so involved in Mario's story she'd tuned out the rest of the world. Probably not a good idea. But Ian hadn't. "What is it?"

"Joseph should have call—" His ringing phone cut him off. He snatched it up. "Joseph, did you find them? I see. Okay, thanks. See you soon."

He hung up. "I don't know how much time we have left. But we still don't have the microchip and Joseph and Catelyn are still searching for these guys that seem to have disappeared. The police are helping, but it's such a small setup that they just don't have the manpower they need. They've called in help from some surrounding counties, but honestly, they're no match for these guys."

Anxiety tightened her stomach and she fiddled with the play button. "We need to finish watching this. He may tell us where it is by the end of the DVD."

"Turn it back on, but be ready to run if I tell you to."

"We can't leave without that microchip. Mario's death can't be for nothing."

He thought for a moment, staring at Mario's paused face on the screen. "I've got an idea."

"What?"

"I'm going to call Mac and ask him for help."

"Do you think that's wise?"

"Guess we'll find out." He held up his phone. "It's ringing."

Mac answered on the second ring. "Masterson, where are you?"

"At a safe place, but I need your help."

"Anything."

"Gina and I are getting close to finding what Mario hid. It's a microchip, but he never had a chance to look at it real well before he was killed. And while he's left us a trail of clues to follow, he hasn't come right out and said where this chip is."

"But you think you can find it?"

"With a little more time and your help, yes, I think so."

"Tell me what you need and I'll make sure you get it."

Ian appreciated the man's willingness. "All right, I need to make sure we're safe. We've figured out Bandit is the traitor in this mess, and we need you to keep him away from here. We can't search constantly looking over our shoulders, waiting for him to show up."

"Not a problem. I can have my guys wherever you need us. Give me your location."

Ian did so, figuring Bandit already knew where they were anyway and was probably on the way out to the farm. Maybe Mac would be able to intercede, and they would have a bit more time to search. "Thanks, Mac, and I'll call you as soon as we find that microchip so you can see that it gets to the proper authorities."

"Will do, Masterson. You're a good man and I'd be glad to have you back on my team anytime you're ready."

"Appreciate that. Gotta go. I'll call you soon."

They hung up and Ian returned to Gina. "I've got two more phone calls to make and I'll be right there. I think everything is going to be just fine."

"You think Mac was the right person to call?"

"I think Mac was the perfect person to call."

NINETEEN

Gina watched Ian pace as he waited for whoever he was calling to answer. Turning back to the DVD, she decided to go ahead and watch and if anything major turned up, she would fill him in.

She pressed Play and Mario came to life once more. A pang filled her as she watched him talk and move. She was so relieved he'd gotten right with God before his death that tears came each time she thought about it. *Thank you, Lord, that he's with You.*

Gina reached up to grasp the necklace, wondering when he'd had time to put the key in it. She thought about some of their last moments together and knew it had been the day they'd gone hiking. He'd taken the necklace from her to examine the picture of his sister.

"She would have loved you, Gina," he'd told her.

And she'd looked into his brown eyes and told him, "I'm sure I would have loved her, too."

He'd put his arm around her, and they'd watched the sun set together. Then he'd left and she hadn't seen him again—until now. She tuned back in to what he was saying.

"I knew Ian would help you. You see, Gina, you were the reason he left the unit. He was in love with you."

She gasped, pressed Pause and, with a pounding heart, whirled to look for Ian. He'd disappeared and she wilted with relief. She looked at Mario, frozen on the screen. "What? Are you crazy?"

Certifiable.

Ian was in love with her? Had been in love with her all this time? He came back in the room and she looked at him, still talking on the phone, pacing from one end to the other. She didn't know what the other person was saying, but Ian looked intense.

Him? In love with her? There was no way that could be possible. Ian wouldn't have left the unit just because of her—would he? *She* was the reason he'd left? It didn't compute.

Flicking the play button, she gathered her composure as she listened to the rest of what Mario had to say.

"So anyway, now you know."

"Know what?" Ian's deep voice rumbled beside her and she jumped.

"Um…nothing. That part wasn't important. Just something personal between Mario and me."

Sympathy softened his eyes. "All right. Would you like to watch the rest of the video by yourself?"

Did she? No, Mario probably wouldn't mention anything again about Ian being in love with her, and they were running out of time. "No, stay. It's fine."

He stood behind her and rested his hands on her shoulders. She shivered and closed her eyes. Should she feel guilty? Maybe. Did she? Not really. Mario had given her the freedom to love again. He'd even picked the guy for her. How ironic.

"I hope you can forgive me, Gina. Everything I did, I did to protect you." He stood and carried the camera from room to room. He zoomed in on various things in each room as though taking inventory—or saying goodbye. "Thank you for loving my grandmother. You brought light back into her life after Patrice died. And she loved this house. I was looking forward to living here again one day." He stopped in Patrice's room, panned around it, then he was back in front of the camera again. "Gina, you were the only woman in her life that didn't disappoint her. Always a picture of true beauty. Anyway, until we meet again." He kissed two fingers and placed them on the lens of the camera. Then it went blank.

And Gina knew she'd truly seen the last of Mario Anthony.

And would bet her last breath there was a last clue hidden somewhere in the video. And she still didn't know what to look for.

Exhausted beyond belief, emotionally wrung out and so frustrated she wanted to scream, she sat back in the chair and stared at the computer.

"Any idea?" Ian asked.

She jerked, then looked up at him and blinked. "No."

Weariness crossed his face and he patted her shoulder. "All right, then, I'll get in contact with Joseph and let him know we just can't find it."

Tears blurred her vision once more. "I'm sorry, Ian. I just…I can't…I don't know!" She threw her hands up in defeat and stood.

He quickly crossed to her side and gathered her close. "It's all right, Gina."

"No, it isn't," she mumbled against his chest, inhaling his sweet male scent. He was in love with her?

She slid her arms around his waist and rested there for one brief, peaceful moment; then it was over. She pulled away. "I'll figure it out. I have to."

He let her go, the longing in his eyes making her heart thump. Oh, boy.

She turned to leave the office and the necklace around her neck flashed a reflection in the mirror on the opposite wall.

And she stopped.

Looked back at the computer screen.

Then back at the mirror.

"What is it?" he asked, eyes sharp and questioning, any trace of emotion gone.

She moved back to the desk. "Can you play the last part of that DVD again? Just the part where Mario's saying goodbye."

"Sure." He clicked the necessary buttons to bring up the disc again, then forwarded to the part she'd requested and pressed Play.

She narrowed her eyes, intent on watching each picture. "Ian, did you hear what he said?"

"About what?"

His phone rang. He looked at the screen and raised a brow. "It's Mac."

"Go ahead and answer it."

She registered Ian's side of the conversation absentmindedly as she thought about her next move and watched the end one more time.

Ian was saying, "No, we haven't found it, but I think if we have about thirty more minutes, we'll have it. Yeah. Yeah. Thanks for the help."

As Mario did his walk-through of the house, the picture of Mario's sister stood out to her this time. He'd zoomed in on the portrait, then out and moved on.

The portrait. It still hung on the wall in his sister's bedroom. The portrait that had been painted two weeks before she'd died. A picture of true beauty.

Reaching into the back pocket of her jeans, she pulled out the now-ratty letter she'd found at the beach house. Scanning through it, she stopped at the part that said, "Grandmother thought the world of you. You're the only woman in her life who didn't disappoint her."

"The only woman in her life who didn't disappoint her. Now that's not true."

"What's not true?"

"I wasn't the only woman in her life that didn't disappoint her. At first I thought Mario must be referring to his mother because of the abandonment. I guess I think of Patrice, his sister, as a child, but maybe Mario included her in this."

"And?"

"I think Mario's giving me another clue here. I think Patrice's portrait has something to do with all this."

"Where is it?"

"Follow me."

Turning on her heel, she led the way down the hall to Patrice's old room. Perfectly preserved, it looked as if it waited on her to return from some teenage jaunt.

And the portrait hung above the bed. A beautiful piece, it captured the girl's gentle spirit and love of life. She looked a lot like Mario. Sadness engulfed Gina as she thought about the brother and sister who'd both died too young.

"Okay, what are we looking for?"

Tears blurred her vision. Had they finally come to the end of this crazy, world-shattering journey?

"I think the microchip is up there." She pointed to the portrait. "Can you help me get it off the wall?"

"Sure." Without question or hesitation, he took his shoes off and stood on the bed to gently remove the painting. "It's heavy."

"Yeah, Mina would have only used the best for her Patrice."

With a grunt, he turned from the wall and bent to let it slide to the floor, letting it lean against the edge of the bed. Then he hopped down, slid back into his shoes and said, "All right, you're up."

"Do you have a pocketknife?"

He slanted her an amused glance and pulled out his Swiss Army knife. "What size blade do you need?"

"The smallest one."

He obliged and handed it over.

"Thanks." With focused concentration, she leaned over the painting and took a deep breath. The small razor-sharp blade hovered over the girl's throat, and with a gentle yet firm movement, Gina inserted the blade just under the locket.

TWENTY

Ian held his hand under the small flap that Gina loosened with the knife, and a tiny object tumbled into his palm. Elation flooded him and he looked up at Gina. "You're amazing. You did it."

She flushed and looked flustered, then shrugged. "Well, if you hadn't kept me alive, I wouldn't have gotten past the beach house." She gave him an intense look, one that burned to the very depths of his heart.

He leaned over and kissed her, gently, a quick touch to her lips that promised so much more. "We've got a lot to talk about later, okay?"

Eyes wide, she nodded. Then he became all business again. "All right, let's get this back in there."

"What?" Confusion wiped the dazed look from her face.

"I still don't know who the good guys are, so we're not taking any chances. I wish I had time to see what's on it, but know we don't. And if the bad guys show up before the good guys, I want to make sure that thing is protected. Can you get it back in there without ruining the picture?"

"Maybe. Mario did a good job gluing the flap back to the painting. I had to get very close to notice it had been disturbed. There's some glue down in the kitchen. I'll just run down there and get some."

He handed her the chip. "I'll do it. Which drawer?"

She told him and he left to get the glue. He also wanted to make a couple of calls. Dialing the first number, he got Joseph. "Did you find them?"

"Negative on that. Catelyn's working with the reinforcements you called in to keep up the search. I'm making sure they've got all the information they need. Then I'll be on my way out to the farm in case you need backup. Did you find what you were looking for?"

"Sure did and I'm making phone calls to make sure I've got all my bases covered."

"Great. Be there shortly."

Ian hung up and made the next call. Mac answered on the first ring. "Did you find it?"

"Yes, sir. I can't tell you how much I appreciate you taking it off our hands like this."

"Have you looked at it? Do you know what it was that made these guys willing to kill for it?"

"No, sir. I haven't had a chance to look at it."

"Might be best if you don't."

"That's kind of how I feel about it. But Mario did leave a DVD behind. He confirmed that Bandit's the one who set him up."

"Bandit? Are you sure? He's been undercover a long time."

Mac sighed heavily. "I hate to hear that."

"Be careful if you run into him. He's here in town somewhere."

"All right, it'll take me a while to get there, but I'm on my way."

"See you soon, sir. I'll be waiting."

Ian hung up the phone with a feeling of satisfaction. Hopefully, this was all about to come to an end and he and Gina would be safe.

Gina watched Ian hang the picture back on the wall. "What do you think is on the chip?" she asked.

Tilting the picture a little more to the left to make it level, he finally turned and shrugged. "I don't know. Some kind of incriminating evidence against someone, I'm sure."

"Someone from the unit?"

"No doubt."

"Can you tell where the chip is?"

Ian studied the painting, then shook his head. "Not really. If I didn't know it was in there, I wouldn't notice it."

"Good."

Ian shoved his gun into the back of his jeans and turned to make his way down the stairs. Gina followed, stepping lightly behind him.

They made their way back into the den, with Ian checking the windows and looking at the clock. "All right, here's the plan," he said.

"Yeah, Ian, tell us the plan."

Gina whirled, gasping as she took in the man who stepped out from behind the door to the den, his gun leveled at the two of them.

Ian pulled Gina behind him and managed to grip the butt of his gun before the weapon in the stranger's hand cracked. Gina screamed as Ian fell back against her, knocking her sideways.

"Ian!" She threw herself down beside him, keeping one eye on the advancing menace in front of her. Ian lay still, eyes closed. The wound in his shoulder bled only a small amount.

Had the bullet passed through?

Was he dead?

Running her hand down his back, she felt for the gun. "What are you doing?" she yelled at the man.

"Reclaiming what's mine." He pointed the gun at her head. "Now where is it?"

"I don't know what you're talking about."

Annoyance flashed across his uneven features. The tattoo on his hand caught her eye; then his words chilled her soul. "Lady, if you don't tell me where it is, the next bullet goes in his head." He moved the gun from her head to Ian's.

And she knew she'd have to tell.

"It's…"

Ian struck, flinging a leg around his opponent's and pulling him to the floor with a crash. The man's gun skittered across the floor and Gina lunged for it.

"Gina, get out!" Ian hollered at her as he took a punch to the gut. Doubled over, he propelled his body forward to head-butt the man on the chin.

Gina hesitated, her fingers wrapped around the unfamiliar weapon. Her hands shook too hard to shoot straight.

But she had to try.

An elbow to Ian's cheek split it and the blood flowed. Handicapped by his wounded shoulder, he appeared to be weakening.

Sucking in a deep breath, she held the gun in front of her just like Joseph had taught her.

And froze when she felt something touch the back of her neck. "Put the gun down, Gina."

Swallowing hard, defiance flowing, she held the gun steady. The pressure on her neck increased as Ian delivered a final punch to an exposed chin. His opponent went down and stayed there, eyes closed. Ian sagged against the fireplace, grasping the mantel to keep himself upright. He turned to find Gina held hostage, a gun to the back of her head.

Gasping, he winced at the damage his body had sustained. Gina trembled, desperate to run to him and make sure he would be all right.

But first they had to deal with the man standing behind her. The voice sounded familiar, but she couldn't place it. Ian kept his eyes steady as they focused on the newcomer.

"Hello, Mac."

TWENTY-ONE

Mac gave Gina a small shove, forcing her farther into the room. "Tell your girlfriend to put down the gun."

Ian eyed Gina, spying the stubborn determination glinting through her terror.

"Gina…"

"No," she blurted, "he's just going to kill us anyway."

"Not if we give him what he wants," Ian lied.

"That's not true and you know it."

She was way too smart for her own good.

"I promised I'd get you out of this. Now listen to me and put the gun down. Trust me."

She trembled, looked deep into eyes that he struggled to keep steady but knew were hazed with pain. Doing his best to ignore it and the weakness surging through him, he stood straight, trying to give the appearance of strength. He needed her to trust him. Desperately.

"Drop it, Gina," Mac ordered from behind her.

The man was losing patience. He could shoot her and still have Ian, who had the information he needed. Of course Ian would be a tougher nut to crack than Gina. In spite of the pain, Ian's mind ticked along, coming up with one scenario, discarding it and forming another. All in the space of seconds.

Mac would use them against each other.

And Ian knew that if Mac threatened Ian, Gina would ll him exactly where the chip was. Truth be told, he dn't know that he wouldn't do the same if Mac contin- :d to threaten Gina. Either way, the man couldn't leave em alive.

Gina lowered the gun gently to the floor. Mac stepped round her and, placing his foot on the weapon, dragged it him. He left it on the floor, never taking his eyes from Ian r the gun from the back of Gina's head.

"What's on the chip, Mac? What is it you and Bandit—" e gestured to the unconscious man on the floor "—are so esperate to keep hidden?"

"It doesn't matter now. Where is it?"

"Surely you know me better than that."

The man kept the gun steady on the back of Gina's neck. His lips parted in a mockery of a smile. "I know that you lon't want to watch this woman die, do you?"

Gina flinched and bit her lip. Ian took a deep breath, shot her what he hoped was a reassuring look, then said in a conversational tone, "You got here faster than I thought you would."

"I was closer than I let on."

Ian had figured that but hadn't counted on the man getting here quite this quick. Glancing at the clock on the wall, he grasped for more time, just a little more time. Sweat wanted to break out across his forehead, but he wouldn't allow himself to show that kind of weakness. "What made you do it, Mac? Money?"

"Yes. Money. Lots and lots of money. I gave my life to this country and for what? A measly little pension when I can't do their dirty work anymore? No, thanks. I've got

Jimmy to take care of, and providing him the kind of ca
he deserves is expensive."

"What happened to honor and integrity? Values that yo
preached to us?"

Remorse flickered briefly, then hardened into resolutio
"Yeah, I used to feel that way. Then one by one my fami
left me until I had no one left but the unit. Then you left an
the unit didn't fall apart, but it was never the same. The guy
just…" He shrugged. "But all that doesn't matter anymore
What matters is that chip. Now hand it over."

"I don't have it."

"But you know where it is."

Ian felt himself growing weaker. Time clicked slowly. Jus
a few more minutes. He had to stay strong, lucid. Finger
gripped the mantel, and he glared at his former superviso
One hand tangled in Gina's curls at the base of her neck; th
other hand gripped the butt of the gun.

Which he now shifted to aim at Ian's heart. Without looking
at Gina, he said, "It's up to you, girl. Does he live or die?"

From the corner of her eye, Gina watched Mac's finger
tighten around the trigger, and nausea churned in her
stomach. Ian kept his gaze steady on her, silently telling her
not to say a word.

But she couldn't let Ian be shot again. He wouldn't
survive it. And even though he held himself steady, he looked
pasty-white.

"It's…"

"Gina, no."

Mac's fingers tightened in the handful of hair and she
blinked at the blinding pain—but refused to cry out. He
yanked her with him as he strode closer to Ian. Tears flowed

down her cheeks, and she had to bite her lip against the scream curling in her throat. Against her ear, he growled, "One more chance—then the bullet goes in his head. Tell me."

"It's in Patrice's room!"

Ian closed his eyes. "Don't do it, Gina. Don't let Mario's death be for nothing."

"Show me." Hand still snarled by her hair, Mac dragged her toward the steps, then looked back at Ian. "I suppose you're ready to fall over, but knowing you, you'd cause me trouble if I just left you here."

He raised the gun toward Ian and Gina gasped, "No, don't shoot him. Let me go get it. Stay here and watch him and let me go get it. I'll come back, I promise."

Mac paused and Bandit stirred. Lightning fast, Ian's foot shot out and clipped the man in the head, sending him back into the darkness from which he'd just tried to awaken.

Growling again, Mac pulled the trigger.

And missed, as Ian hit the floor next to Bandit, then rolled. Mac aimed again and, ignoring the scorching pain coming from her scalp, Gina screamed, "Stop it! Stop it! I'll get it!"

Mac stopped and focused his attention back on her, eyes narrowed in anger, cold chips from the depths of the Arctic. "Do it." He gave her a shove toward the stairs, and Gina stumbled to keep her balance.

Ian locked his gaze on hers. Run, he was silently shouting—get out as soon as you can.

As if.

But she would try to get some help. Somewhere, somehow. She whirled up the stairs, desperately seeking a way out. A weapon, a phone to call for help.

No doubt Mac had cut the nonworking phone line as a precaution, but that wouldn't have helped her anyway. She made it to the top of the stairs and turned left, making her way down the hallway and stopping in front of Patrice's room.

"I'm waiting!" Mac called from below.

"I'm coming! It's hidden really well." Under her breath, she muttered, "Joseph, Joseph, where are you?"

She raced to the window in Patrice's room and looked down at the drive.

Empty.

The sound of a helicopter reached her but she ignored it, going straight to the painting on the wall. Sliding a fingernail under the edge she'd just recently glued back into place, she lifted it and the chip fell into her outstretched palm. Shaking, she tucked the reason for all her problems into the front pocket of her jeans.

Her eyes fell on the pack Ian had brought into the room with him earlier. She fell to her knees and grabbed it. It took her trembling fingers three tries, but she finally got it unzipped. She pulled the laptop out and put it aside. Then she dumped the thing upside down. All kinds of interesting gadgets poured out, but the one thing she was most interested in tumbled to the floor with a thump.

A camera.

They should be here by now. Nausea clawed at his throat. Pain from his wound radiated and his knees felt like rubber. The clock ticked, the second hand creeping its way around the numbers. Where were they?

The man in front of him looked calm, unruffled, as though he did this on a daily basis—held people at gunpoint and planned to kill them as soon as he got what he wanted.

And maybe he did.

Ian certainly didn't know who Mac was anymore.

"Who else is in on your little game?"

"Game?" The gun shook and Mac's nostrils flared. "Oh, this is no game, Ian. No game."

"Right. So who else is involved? Jase?"

A snort escaped the man. "Not likely. He's like you. Thinks everything is black and white, right or wrong. He can't see the shades of gray."

Relief chugged through Ian. His instincts had been right after all. "Good, I'm glad to hear it."

"Unfortunately, Jase will have to suffer a similar fate to Mario. He knows too much, is asking too many questions—thanks to you and Gina."

One more reason he needed to fight off the weakness that was almost overwhelming. He knew if he looked at his knuckles, they'd be bleached white with the effort it took to keep his grip on the mantel.

"Let me call him. I'll tell him to back off, that everything's fine. There's no need to kill him, too."

"I don't think so." His eyes flicked to the steps. "Now, where's Gina? You don't suppose she's run off, do you?"

Ian could only hope. Unfortunately, he didn't think so. What *was* taking her so long?

The helicopter thumping in the distance shot adrenaline through him, sharpening his senses, sending a surge of strength he desperately needed. Straightening his spine, he hissed at the bolt of pain that lanced him. Managing to ignore it, he glanced at Bandit, still out cold on the floor.

"Wake him up," Mac ordered.

"What?"

"Wake him up!" He looked back at the stairs. "Gina! You better be down here in thirty seconds with that chip!"

The thumping of the helicopter sounded closer. This

time Mac noticed it. Eyes narrowed in fury, he shouted, "Who is it?"

"The good guys, I'm hoping." Satisfaction warred with worry. The cavalry might be on the way, but Mac still had time to kill them, a fact that Mac wasn't unaware of.

He lifted the gun.

"Here!" Gina's breathless voice sounded from the bottom of the steps. She held out the chip. "Just take it and go. Please! I don't care what's on there. I don't care what you're involved in. Just go!"

Mac snatched the item from her outstretched fingers and slid it into his pocket even as he backed toward the door. "You knew, didn't you? That phone call you made, asking me to help gain you more time. You knew I'd hold off on coming out here until you called to tell me you'd found it."

"Yeah. I was hoping I was wrong, but when Bandit didn't show up as quick as I'd expected, I figured you'd told him to stand down to give us time to find it."

And then Mac knew he was out of time. The gun lifted and Ian shouted, "Gina, trust me. Run!"

TWENTY-TWO

Without thought or hesitation, Gina pulled the camera from behind her back, lifted it and pressed the button. The flash sparked right in Mac's eyes, blinding him for a brief moment.

Then she turned and bolted for cover.

Ian staggered from the mantel and lunged to clip Mac's legs, but the man was too strong for Ian in his weakened state and easily pulled away. Mac aimed his weapon.

Ian rolled.

Mac fired.

Then he slipped out the door.

Gina raced to Ian, who lay still on the floor. "Are you okay?"

He winced and struggled to his feet, swaying, ignoring the pain. "Yeah, hand me that gun."

Gina didn't hesitate. She grabbed the weapon and handed it to Ian. He weaved his way out the door, gun gripped in his right hand. "Stay here."

"What are you doing?"

"I can't let him get away."

She followed him to the door. At that moment, an SUV came barreling across the field toward the house. Ian stumbled in the direction he thought Mac may have headed but didn't get far before he went down on one knee. Gina ran to Ian's side and shoved a shoulder under his armpit grateful he was alive. So grateful they were both alive.

Joseph jumped out and raced over to the two of them and wrapped an arm around Ian. He helped Gina heft him back to his feet. "Where is he?"

"I'm not sure. He ran out of here a few minutes ago. He can't have gotten far. What took you so long, man?"

Joseph motioned for the other men in the vehicle to give chase. They did and he started explaining, "I ran into Robbie Stillman and had to take care of him."

Ian grunted. "Bet that went over well."

"He definitely didn't want to be taken care of. It took a lot of convincing."

"Is that how you got that nice shiner?"

Joseph grimaced. "Yeah. The sheriff made it in time to help me out, but not before Robbie got in a good punch. Stings like mad."

"I know what you mean." Between Gina and Joseph, they managed to maneuver Ian back into the house, where he dropped to the couch and stayed there. Bandit had been cuffed and removed from the premises.

"Where's Catelyn?" Gina asked even as she headed for the kitchen to gather supplies to take care of Ian's wound until the ambulance could get there.

Joseph raised his voice so she could hear. "She's with the sheriff trying to get as much information out of Robbie as she can."

Ian huffed out a painful chuckle. "You won't get anything out of him."

"Yeah, we realize that, but we can get on his nerves for a while. At least until we find something that will allow us to put him away."

This time Ian groaned and leaned his head back against the couch cushion. "Ugh. Mac has the microchip—and any evidence we might have had."

"Um, not exactly," Gina murmured.

Ian's eyes popped open and Joseph's swiveled in her direction. She set the first aid materials on the coffee table and said, "I didn't give him the chip."

A frown creased Ian's forehead. "What do you mean? I watched you do it."

She shrugged. "I took a chance and gave him the media card from the camera. I didn't figure he'd take the time to look at it too closely—or recognize it if he did. Thankfully, he just stuck it in his pocket." She shuddered at the remembered terror. "So now what? He's still out there, and as soon as he has a chance to look at that camera card, he's going to realize I gave him the wrong thing. Then he'll just be back and we'll start this all over again." Her voice rose in frustration.

Joseph's jaw clenched. "That's why we're going to get him before that happens."

"Absolutely," Ian concurred. "Now, give me a phone. I've got to call Jase and warn him to be on the lookout for Mac. Also, we need a unit to keep an eye on the Rodriguez family. Mac may try to go there for protection."

Joseph grunted. "He won't be going by plane. I've got teams at the three closest airports with Mac's picture everywhere. I've also got something going to the TV stations with his picture. If by some crazy way he somehow does get back to Colombia, he's a dead man. Once old Esteban realizes Mac's got the wrong thing, he'll kill him."

Ian couldn't argue with that statement.

* * *

While Gina watched ambulance personnel arrive and begin to work on Ian, Joseph stood outside the door strategizing. Unable to convince Ian to go to the hospital, the paramedics patched him up as well as they could.

"It's just a flesh wound," he assured them. "The bullet passed out the other side. It's painful, but I don't think it's done much damage, if any." The young paramedic agreed with Ian's assessment but declared an X-ray necessary to be sure.

Gina tried to get Ian to go with them, but he was adamant. "I'm going after Mac. I'll let someone look at it when that man's in custody."

"But, Ian, you don't have any idea where he'd go, do you?"

He looked away. "No, not a clue. And if our guys haven't caught up with him yet, he had a vehicle stashed somewhere."

Joseph nodded. "We never spotted one, not from the air or the ground. He had it hidden well. Under some trees or in a nearby building. It doesn't matter now. All that matters is catching up with him." His phone rang and he excused himself. Gina prayed it was news that Mac had been captured.

Catelyn was still occupied with the sheriff and Robbie Stillman, who still hadn't cracked. Ian had called his current commander, who agreed to fly in and take the chip off their hands and turn it in to the appropriate authorities. Carly had called to check in, and when Ian hadn't explained what was going on, Gina had taken the phone from him and spilled everything. He told her to keep an eye out for his sister as he felt sure she'd probably show up before too long.

He reached for Gina's hand and her insides trembled as his fingers curled around hers. She swallowed hard. "You scared me, Ian."

Intense eyes bored holes into hers. "You trusted me."

She swallowed. "I had to."

"You'll never know what that means to me."

Joseph reentered the room and shoved his phone in his pocket with a disgusted sigh. "We lost Mac. Unless you can come up with an idea of where he might head…"

Ian stood, his face twisting into a painful grimace. Keeping his arm tucked against his side, he paced to the door and back as he thought and muttered, "Where would he go?"

Joseph shrugged. "If he goes home, we've got guys covering his house."

"No, he won't go home. Surely, he prepared for this. Had some kind of backup plan in case he failed. That was practically his motto. 'If you have a plan A, B and C, make sure you have a D, E and F,'" he quoted. "He's got a plan. I just don't know what it would be."

Gina watched the men brainstorm as Ian paced. The fluids the paramedics had given him seemed to have infused him with renewed strength and energy. She wondered how long that would last.

Hopefully long enough.

Ian clapped his hands together, then winced. "All right, my first guess says that he'll want to find a place to check out what's on that chip, so let's head toward the town. Where would be a good place to find a computer and be inconspicuous about it?"

Gina spoke up. "The library."

"Good idea. I can't see him stopping at any of them, but we can't take the chance. Let's get someone covering all the libraries in town."

"What about the three universities in town? They all have computer labs."

"Tracking him down may be impossible." But Ian picked

up his phone anyway and made the arrangements. When he hung up, he said, "So far the bases I've covered are his home, his office at the base in Georgia, the local libraries, the universities and everywhere else they think he might land. They're even sending a team back to Colombia to watch Rodriguez just in case Mac has a private plane stashed somewhere and manages to get out of the country."

The trio made their way to Joseph's car, and Gina wondered if this day would ever end.

Joseph and Ian took the front, with Joseph behind the wheel—much to Ian's obvious frustration. "You're not driving with that arm," was all Joseph said.

Gina climbed in the back.

Inspiration kicked Ian like a punch to the nose just on the edge of town. "His son."

Gina leaned forward. "What about his son?"

Excitement chased away the weariness that had descended over Ian during the thirty-minute drive. "He won't go anywhere without his son. Mac's going to have to get out of the country to escape prosecution and jail. There's no way he can hide out here in the United States with a special-needs adult like Jimmy."

"You think he'll try to take Jimmy with him?" Joseph asked.

"I know it. Mac loves that kid and would never leave him behind for as long as he's going to have to be gone for. Jimmy may just be Mac's one emotional weakness." He looked at Joseph. "Take us to the airport. I'll arrange for the chopper to meet us there. It's the only way we'll be able to beat Mac to the home where Jimmy lives."

"We're only about twenty minutes from the airport."

Ian paused. "The only problem is we're not going to be

able to sneak up on him. We'll have to land a couple of miles out. And I'll have to arrange to have a car there, too." Thinking out loud, he muttered, "No, by the time we do all that, Mac will already be there—he's got about an hour's head start depending on how fast he's driving and whether he has to stop for gas or anything."

"Then we'll have to drive it," Joseph determined.

"You're right. We will. I can arrange a team to be there to keep an eye on things, but they'll have to stay out of sight. I don't have a good feeling about Mac's mental state right now."

Gina asked, "You think he might do something to hurt his son?"

"No, I don't think he would hurt Jimmy, but another resident to get Jimmy out of there? I just don't know, but I don't want to get into a hostage situation."

"No, we don't want that."

"I'll call and have them lock down the place. We have to protect the residents and staff first. Then we'll figure out how to go about grabbing Mac."

Ian got on the phone to get the number to the home. Once he had that, he carried out his plans, arranging for a team to be there, and prepared to handle whatever situation might arise. "Call me back and let me know what's going on," he told the leader of the unit assigned to the home.

They rode in silence for a good while until Joseph asked, "Now, what do we do with Gina?"

Ian turned in his seat to look at her, a speculative look in his eye. "She'll have to stay in the car. We don't have time to drop her anywhere." He asked her, "Can we trust you stay in the car, or do I need to find an officer to keep an eye on you?"

"Hey! That was uncalled for. I'll stay out of trouble, I promise."

His eyes narrowed. "Hmm."

Joseph gave a low chuckle, then said, "You know her pretty well, don't you?"

Gina reached up and gave Joseph's head a light smack. "Zip it, big brother."

Ian's phone rang, cutting off any response Joseph might have had to his sister's admonition. Ian answered it halfway through the first ring. Jase. "What do you have?"

"You called it. Mac's already there. He's in his son's home. Everything looks peaceful right now. And nothing to indicate Mac's in a hurry."

Ian thought. "No, I remember him saying something about how Jimmy was so laid-back it drove him crazy sometimes. Most of the time Jimmy goes at his own pace, although he can occasionally have a ferocious temper that even Mac has trouble dealing with. Right now, let's hope he stays calm. This might work in our favor." He looked at his watch. "All right, just keep an eye on things. Don't let Mac know you're there unless you have to in order to keep him from leaving. We're about ten minutes away."

They'd already crossed the Georgia state line. The home was just beyond the border. The miles clicked by, and soon Joseph turned down the street that led to the group home.

A uniformed officer stood at the entrance to the street. Joseph pulled to a stop and rolled down his window. The officer leaned in and said, "License check."

Joseph and Ian flashed their badges. The man would have been informed of who to look for. Everyone else would have been turned back and rerouted away from the area.

The officer stepped back and waved them on.

Six group homes—built by a private donor, according to Mac—lined the small cul-de-sac.

One way in. One way out.

Mac's black truck sat outside the home at the top of the circle. Backed into the drive and ready to go.

Joseph parked across the street, hiding the car from the view of the group home, yet positioning so that he could see it from the driver's seat. Ian turned to Gina. "Stay put, please?"

Worried dark eyes stared up at him. "Be careful."

"I will."

She turned to Joseph. "You, too."

He nodded his promise and the two men turned to head over to the man in charge of the team in place. Strategically placed members stayed out of sight but within range of the house.

Joseph spoke up. "All right, how do you want to handle this? You know the guy—I'll follow your lead."

"I honestly don't know that talking to him is going to get us anywhere. Is anyone else in the house?"

"Just the director."

"Do we have a negotiator on standby?" Ian took the binoculars from Joseph and tried to see into the house. Closed blinds blocked his view.

"Yep."

"All right." He tossed the binoculars aside. "I say let's wait until they come out and get in the truck. Let him think he's getting away clean. I definitely don't want to get into a car chase with him, though, so we need to make sure we can get to him before he tries to go anywhere."

"We need to separate him from Jimmy as soon as we can."

A female SWAT team member approached with more equipment. "Here. This will allow you to hear everything going on. The other five houses on the cul-de-sac are on lockdown. No one's getting on or off this street. We've been instructed to go on your command, sir."

Ian thanked her and shoved the earpiece in. He looked at the truck, sitting innocently in the driveway, and wondered how long they had until Mac decided to leave.

"What if we dismantle the truck?" he suggested to Joseph.

"Can you do it without being seen?"

Ian pushed his sleeve up, ignoring the pulsing throb still emanating from his wounded arm. "That's the question of the decade. It's right in front. If he walks out that door…"

"Yeah, you're a sitting duck."

With the car window down, Gina could hear every word the men said as they discussed their strategy. Antsy, wishing there was something, anything, she could do to help, she watched the house for any sign of movement. Then she saw Ian sneaking toward the truck.

She reached for the door handle, wanting to shout at him to get back where it was safe. But she bit her lip and slid from the car to stand beside it. Positioned just right, she had a better view of the situation. And she would be able to stay out of trouble as she'd promised.

The door to the house flew open, and Gina gasped as Ian froze, ducking low behind the truck he'd not yet managed to disable.

"No, not going," the young man yelled over his shoulder as he stomped down the front steps. "My home—this is my home. Not going right now. Sorry."

Mac followed close behind, as did the director of the house. A Mr. Gibson, they'd been told. Gina saw Ian and Joseph exchange a glance. They hadn't alerted the director to what Mac was planning, worried that he would act out of character and tip Mac off. The fifty-something man was saying,

'Jimmy, wait. I'm sure your dad means you're just going away for a while. Not forever." He looked at Mac. "Right?"

Mac ran a hand over his short cropped hair. "Yeah, right, Jimmy, just for a little while."

Jimmy stopped, then asked in a choppy, stilted voice, "Then why do I have to pack all of my clothes?"

"You don't. Just bring a few shirts and pants, then."

Jimmy seemed to have to stop and think about that one. "But it's almost Christmas. I have to help wrap the presents. Have to help, Dad. Can't leave now."

"Jimmy…"

"Go away, Dad. Come back later."

"I can't, Jimmy. I need you to come with me today. Now get in the truck. I'll let you change the gears."

That seemed to tempt the boy trapped in an adult's body. He paused and his eyes lit up. "Drive and Reverse?"

"Sure, buddy, sure. And even Neutral if you want. Just get in the truck, all right?" Desperation stamped Mac's face.

Gina saw what Mac couldn't see. Ian was trapped on the passenger's side. If Jimmy walked around to get in, he'd see Ian—and bring attention to his presence.

But maybe Joseph could move in fast enough to grab Mac before Jimmy said anything about Ian.

Jimmy finally shook his head. "No, I want to wrap the presents. That's important. My job. I want to stay here."

Mac looked ready to chew nails. Mr. Gibson placed a hand on Mac's arm. "Maybe we should all go back inside and wait until Jimmy calms down a bit. He's upset right now and if you try to push him, you know what's going to happen."

"Yeah, yeah, I do and I don't have time for a temper tantrum." Mac's nervousness seemed to increase, his movements agitated and quick.

"Come on," Mr. Gibson encouraged.

"No, I've drugged him before—I'll do it again. We've got to get moving."

Gina felt sick, wanting to burst from her hiding place and confront Mac. Drug him? Mr. Gibson didn't think much of the idea either if the look on his face was anything to go by.

Ian said something into his radio and shook his head. Telling them not to shoot Mac, she thought. He was too close to Jimmy.

Jimmy stomped past his father, and Mac reached out to grab his arm. "Get. In. The. Truck."

"No." Jimmy jerked his arm from Mac's grip and stumbled away.

"Jimmy, you don't know what you're doing."

Ignoring his father, Jimmy rounded the side of the truck and stopped, tennis shoes squeaking on the concrete. "Who are you?"

TWENTY-THREE

Ian stared at the young man, his mind clicking at warp speed on how to handle this situation.

He placed a finger to his lips in the universal sign for silence. Jimmy cocked his head, his anger fleeing in the surprise of Ian's unexpected presence.

"What'd you say, Jimmy? What are you looking at?" Mac's voice came around the side of the vehicle, and Ian did the only thing he could.

He rolled underneath the truck.

The SWAT team waited, Ian knew, for his order. But there was no way he wanted to utter the command that would result in Mac's being shot in front of his son.

Not if it could be avoided.

If it couldn't...

"Jimmy, what are you doing?" Mac demanded.

"The man."

"What?" Impatience now dripped from Mac. "Get in the car, boy, or I'm going to give you a shot."

Ian cringed. He'd heard how afraid Jimmy was of needles.

"No!" the boy shouted. "No shots. Shots bad."

"Then get in the truck!"

His voice barely above a whisper, Ian spoke into his mic, "Get the son out of the way."

"I got him."

Ian swung his foot out from under the truck and connected with Mac's ankle. The man hollered as his leg went out from under him. He went down—hard, his head smacking the side of the truck.

Jimmy's frightened yell barely registered as Ian rolled from under the vehicle to confront an enraged Mac. Blood ran down the side of his face from the gash on his cheek. Ian rolled once more, landing faceup and ignoring the pulsing pain from his arm. From the corner of his eye, he saw Mac's boot coming toward his head, and he ducked and lunged, grasping the swinging foot and twisting.

With a yell, Mac landed on the hard concrete one more time.

"Dad! Dad!"

Ian heard Jimmy's frantic holler for his father and knew one of the team must have him. He didn't have time to check. Mac came at him, fists clenched. The man swung and clipped Ian in his wounded shoulder.

Pain radiated and he lost his footing but managed a solid punch to Mac's uninjured cheek before stumbling to the side, fighting to get his breath. "I've got a clear shot," he heard in his earpiece. "Permission to…"

"No," he gasped. "Don't shoot him."

Mac spun toward him and Ian braced himself. Using his good arm, he pulled a Taser from his back pocket and held it out of sight. He'd grabbed the nonlethal weapon at the last minute, praying he could use it as an alternative to deadly force. "Stop, Mac. Don't do it."

The man weaved on his feet and shook his head. "I won't survive in jail, Ian. Let them shoot me."

"What about Jimmy?"

Regret flashed briefly; then he said, "He'll be fine."

"Give it up."

"Not a chance." And he lunged.

Ian stood stock-still and waited. At the last minute he whipped his arm around in front of him and let Mac run full tilt into the Taser.

Mac jerked, surprise twisting his features as his body went stiff, then fell to the ground.

And it was over.

Breathing hard, Ian looked up. Gina stood across the street, hands against her mouth. Slowly they dropped to her side. Police rushed in to cuff Mac before he regained his senses.

Jimmy still struggled against the hands that held him. Joseph had grabbed him as soon as Ian's foot had knocked Mac off balance. He'd kept Jimmy facing away from the action so he couldn't watch what was happening.

Relief flooded Ian. At least Jimmy wouldn't remember the vision of his dad having a Taser used on him and being handcuffed.

Once Mac was in custody, Gina slowly made her way through the chaos that now filled the street and the front yard of the house. She stopped in front of Ian. "Are you all right?"

"I think so. Are you?"

"You scared me…again."

"I thought you were going to stay in the car."

She shrugged. "I stayed out of trouble. Let's let that be enough."

He felt a smile curve his lips. Yes, she had stayed out of trouble. He had a feeling that might be a rare event. Ian held out a hand.

That was all the invitation she needed. She didn't hesitate, but threw herself against him, wrapping her arms around him in a bear hug and nearly squeezing the breath from him. He grunted. "You're stronger than you look."

Gina let go and looked up at him, tears hanging on her lashes. He lifted a thumb to catch the wetness that clung precariously. "Hey, what is it? I'm fine. You're fine. The bad guys are wrapped up tight. Mac's going to jail and..."

"Masterson!"

Ian looked up. Mac sat in the back of the cruiser, defeat shouting from his slumped shoulders to his bowed head. The officer getting ready to shut the door paused and looked over at Ian as though asking what he should do.

Ian walked over to Mac. The officer stepped back and allowed Ian some room. Placing a hand on the roof of the car, he leaned over the open window. "Yeah?"

Mac lifted his head and stared at Ian with flat eyes. "I'm a dead man, you know."

Ian felt Gina walk up beside him. Anger flooded him and he shot his former commander a snarl of disgust. "Better you than her."

Mac's gaze flickered only momentarily to Gina. "It was never personal."

She snorted. "Well, it sure felt personal. Excuse me if I don't say, 'Don't worry about it. It's all right.'"

Mac nodded. "Fair enough."

Shifting to allow Gina to see in a little better, Ian placed a hand on her shoulder. Mac still stared at him, so Ian asked, "You have something else on your mind?"

The man cleared his throat. "Uh. Yeah. You know I don't have any family left."

"Right, you mentioned that."

Mac's eyes went to the door of the group house, where

his son had just been taken inside. "Jimmy doesn't have anyone now."

Ian narrowed his eyes and wondered if this was going where he thought it was.

Mac blew out a sigh. "Will you check on him every once in a while? Make sure he's all right? Make sure—" his throat bobbed "—they don't get to him?"

Gina placed a hand over Ian's and he looked at her. She nodded. "It's not his fault his dad is…who he is."

"Yeah," Ian promised. "I'll do it." And he would. Jimmy didn't deserve to suffer for his father's actions.

Mac nodded. No words of thanks passed his lips.

Ian slapped the hood of the car and the officer drove off.

Gina slipped an arm around Ian's waist and he squeezed her shoulder. "Let's get out of here."

TWENTY-FOUR

Gina settled a gently snoring Stefano in his crib and turned to Marianna, signing, "He's so beautiful."

Marianna grinned, her dimples creasing her cheeks, dark eyes dancing. "I know," she signed back as the two walked from the room. "He's such a great baby. But I don't want to talk about him."

"You don't?" Gina feigned shock.

"No, I want to know about you and Ian."

Gina figured that's what her sister wanted to talk about. She sighed. "He's a good man. I like him."

"I think you more than like him." Marianna's hands moved fluently, grace in motion.

Gina grimaced. "Okay. I like him—a lot." And she'd told him so before he left. He'd kissed her goodbye with a promise to return.

Her sister swatted at her, and Gina grinned as she ducked. They made themselves comfortable on the couch and Marianna started to continue her interrogation when the lamp on the end table started flashing in a smooth off-and-on flicker.

Marianna answered the door, the specially rigged doorbell doing its duty for the deaf person inside.

Catelyn entered and Gina gave a mental groan. She was trapped. Signing and speaking at the same time, she accused without heat, "This was a setup."

Catelyn smiled and also signed while speaking, "Not really. I know Ian had to leave for a mission almost as soon as he was done filling out the paperwork on Mac."

Sympathy flashed on the other woman's face. "I know, but I have some information to share about the microchip you found."

"Did you find out what was on it?"

"I did."

Eagerly, Gina leaned forward. "Well?"

Catelyn slid onto the sofa and Marianna took the chair in the corner, where she'd have a good view of the conversation. Catelyn said, "All kinds of names and dates, transactions, future meetings, etcetera. If he admitted he lost the chip, he'd be dead meat. As a result, the authorities are running stings left and right before everyone finds out they have the information they have." She gave a wicked smile. "The good part is, Esteban Rodriguez didn't tell anyone he lost that little chip."

"Was Mac specifically named on there?"

"Yes, along with Robbie Stillman and Bandit McGuire." Gina shuddered at the memories. "I'm just glad it's all over."

"Now, let's pray Ian is home for Christmas."

Ian stared down at Mario's grave, thinking about two men he'd once admired. His heart thrilled that Mario was in heaven with the God he'd known all his life but had just accepted as his Savior shortly before his death.

But he couldn't help the sorrow stirring in his soul at the thought of Mac's future in jail. But the man had made his choices in life. Unfortunately, he'd caved to greed, the lure of money more powerful than the ethics he'd preached as a young commanding officer.

Gina came to stand beside him, her gaze on Mario's marker, her question about another man. "Why did he do it, Ian? What made him change? Mac used to be a man I respected so much. I never would have imagined him turning into such a monster."

Ian placed an arm around her shoulders and brought her close to his side. He'd made it safely home the night before. She snuggled up against him.

"I don't know, Gina. I guess when we get so caught up in the things of this world, we forget it's only temporary. That we're here on this earth for such a short time."

"I know. You're right, of course. I just…" She shook her head. "He killed Mario. He called him back here, set up that training exercise and rigged that bomb to explode."

"Yeah, he did. And he actually set us up a few days ago when he met us out on the road. I should have put it together then." He shook his head in disgust. "But all I could think about was getting that information Mac was bringing about Mario and getting you to safety. Instead, I made us sitting ducks."

She sucked in a deep breath and blinked back tears. "Don't worry about that. When you trust someone, you can be blind to other things." She changed the subject. "Will Jase get in trouble for digging around in the files to get that information for us? The stuff that was on the chip?"

"We didn't ask him to do that."

"I know. I think he felt guilty for taking those pictures of Mario and that woman and accusing Mario of being unfaithful to me."

"Probably, but he'll heal in time. As long as no one knows he messed with Mac's computer, he'll be fine."

She gazed at the clouds. "I'm glad Mario's finally at peace."

"Me, too."

Ian gave her one last squeeze and said, "Are you ready to go for a little drive?"

She looked up at him, curiosity chasing the shadows from her dark eyes. "Sure, where to?"

"Well, it is Christmas Day."

Gina laughed, her eyes crinkling at the corners. "I'm aware of that, thank you."

"And your house is bare."

She blinked in confusion, and he laughed. "Come on."

Two hours later, surrounded by the scent of pine and cold, Gina gasped, laughed and threw the ax down onto the snow-encrusted ground. "You're crazy. I can't do this."

"That's because you have to stop laughing," Ian said. "Who can chop down a tree while giggling?"

Good-natured humor made his eyes twinkle in a way she'd never seen before. It made her heart sing, her blood hum, her stomach flip somersaults. "Then you do it. You keep cracking jokes and expect me to keep a straight face. I can't do it."

He shook his head in mock disgust and picked up the ax. Three more whacks and the tree started creaking. "Timber!" he yelled at the top of his lungs.

And Gina cracked up again. "Thank goodness there's no one here to laugh at you."

"No, I get enough of that from you."

With efficient movements, he picked up the tree he'd tied up mummy-style before cutting, and hefted it to his shoulder, wincing only a little at the reminder he was still healing.

Gina sobered a bit, then grinned as he stomped to the

truck he'd purchased two days earlier. He settled the tree into the back, then walked over to open the door for Gina.

She climbed in and he rounded the front to get into the driver's seat. Ian started the truck and sat there, letting the warm air blast from the heaters. "What do you think about my job, Gina?"

"What?"

The serious turn of his thoughts startled her.

He looked at her. "My job. Is it something you can live with?"

She frowned, sighed and bit her lip. "Why are you asking?"

"Because I want to tell you why I left the unit and I'm feeling a little—insecure. If I knew that you could live with what I do, it would make…what I want to say…um…a little easier."

"Ah. Well." She looked away for a moment.

He squirmed. "What does that mean?"

"It means after Mario was killed, I made a promise to myself."

Dread coated his stomach. "What was that?"

"I promised myself I would never again love someone with a dangerous job. No more Rangers, no cops, no firemen, not even a schoolteacher."

"I see." So he'd lost her. He'd never really had her and he'd already lost her. Pain shafted him.

"And then I met you—again," her soft voice caressed his wounded heart, easing the hurt, making him sit up and pay attention to what she was saying.

"What are saying, Gina?"

"It means I know why you left the unit."

All movement ceased. "Oh."

"Mario told me on the DVD."

He frowned. Surely he would have remembered that part. "Where was I?"

"On the phone trying to save our lives."

"Right." His heart thudded against his ribs. Throughout this whole ordeal, he'd been getting vibes and signals that she cared for him, wanted to grow closer to him. But now she seemed impossible to read, her face not blank but carefully neutral.

And she knew why he left the unit.

Poor guy. She wasn't stringing him along on purpose, she just wanted to make sure she said the right words. Excitement tingled in the pit of her stomach at what she saw developing between them. "I loved Mario."

He winced but nodded, understanding flashing as his hands tightened on the steering wheel. "I know you did, Gina."

"But not like I love you, Ian."

He was still nodding, but all of a sudden he stopped. His eyes latched onto hers and he searched them. He was wondering if he'd heard her right, so she smiled—a shaky parting of her lips. "Yeah, I said it."

He blinked. "I didn't dream it?"

She laughed. "No, Ian, you didn't dream it. I love you."

"When?"

"When what?"

"When did you decide that?"

"The day we were at the farmhouse looking for the microchip."

She reached up and cupped his cheek. He needed a shave but she didn't care. "Mario said you left because you fell in love with me."

He narrowed his eyes. "Yeah."

Tears filled her. What had she done to deserve this man? "I'm sorry."

He leaned forward and touched his forehead to hers. "I love you, Gina Santino."

"And I think I have more respect for you now than ever before. I can't think of another man who would put his career on the line, alienate his best friends and go through what you must have gone through to keep your integrity."

He closed his eyes, then opened them and looked away. She saw the glint of tears. "I had to. I love the Lord more."

Gina threw her arms around his neck and pulled him in for a mind-blowing kiss. Ian sighed and transferred his kisses to her nose and her eyes and finally settled back on her lips.

When he pulled back, he looked down at her and shivered at the love shining there. He said, "You're precious to me, I just want you to know that. I won't take your love for granted."

Speechless, she nodded, then found her voice. "And I vow to do the same."

"We fought too hard to stay alive and reach this point to mess it up."

"Absolutely."

He kissed her again, his gaze longing, wistful—joyous. "Now, are you ready to go decorate a tree?"

She giggled. "Sure."

They arrived at her house right after lunch with only one stop for a burger and fries.

Pulling in the driveway, Ian climbed out and Gina did the same. Clapping her hands against the cold, she looked at her small house. All evidence of trauma had been erased. Christmas lights blinked from her gutters, and two lighted mechanical reindeer grazed on the brown grass. The snow covering the mountain where they'd cut down the tree hadn't made it down to the city of Spartanburg. No white Christmas this year.

Gina hurried to open the door while Ian pulled the tree from the back of the truck. He carried it through the door he held open for him.

"Thanks."

With a grunt, he set it into the tree stand Gina had set up in the corner next to the window.

"You're right. My house is bare. I decorated the outside a bit but not the inside. I just didn't feel like it, I guess." She laughed. "Normally I have everything done a few days after Thanksgiving. It seems a bit of a waste to decorate on Christmas Day."

He stopped what he was doing and looked up. "A waste? How do you figure?"

She shrugged and handed him the scissors. He cut the rope holding the limbs in place. The branches sprung free with what Gina would have sworn was a sigh of relief.

"I don't know. Aren't you supposed to decorate a month or two before?"

Laughing, he said, "So we're starting our own tradition."

A shiver danced through her. Building traditions with Ian sounded wonderful.

"You got the lights and the ornaments?" he asked.

"Right here."

She handed him the string of lights first.

"I like your family," he stated.

"They like you."

He stopped again and looked at her. "Are you sure you don't regret selling the farm?"

She paused in her efforts to untangle the last strand of multicolored lights and smiled. "No, I don't regret it. Mario was the last of his family. A donation in his name to the people fighting crime in Colombia? Yeah, I think that would make him very happy. It was the right thing to do."

He pulled her close for a quick hug. "I'm glad."

Clearing her throat, she asked, "So, are you ready for the ornaments yet?"

He grinned, blue eyes twinkling. "Yep. Why don't you pick out the ones you want to hang? And we'll save mine for last. I brought a special one."

She cocked her head. "To celebrate our first Christmas together?"

A mysterious smile pulled at his lips. "Something like that. Now hang." He handed her a miniature nativity, and she placed it gently on the tree. One by one they hung the ornaments, Gina stopping every once in a while to explain the significance of each fragile piece. Finally, they were all done.

Except for one.

Ian grasped the last ornament and handed it to her. She turned to hang it on the tree, and he saw her pause, heard her gasp, "Oh, Ian." She pulled it to her for closer inspection. His stomach twisted in knots; he decided a mission in the middle of the desert facing down terrorists was less stressful than waiting on her reaction.

"Oh, my," she breathed. "When did you have this done?" She spun the clear glass ornament in front of her eyes. But it wasn't the ornament itself, it was what lay on a purple cushion within. "It's gorgeous."

"You're not mad I didn't let you pick it out?"

"No, of course not. When did you do this? How do I…" She held it out to him.

He took it and with a deft twist, popped off the glass top

d exposed the simple, single-karat diamond set in white ld. "On the flight to our last mission. I made a phone call a friend of mine who's a jeweler. He had it waiting for me en I landed back home." He took it from its resting place d got down on one knee.

Taking her left hand in his, he said, "I love you, Gina. I ink you're amazing and I would be proud to have you as y wife. I know it's kind of fast so if you need some time think about it, that's okay, but would you marry me?"

Gina felt as though the breath had been sucked from her ngs. Then with a wobbly smile, she placed a kiss on his ps. "Ian Masterson, you're the one that's amazing. You ved my life, and you make me laugh. I would be honored be your wife."

His lips settled on hers, and she kissed him back with all e love she had bursting in her heart. He pulled back and aned his forehead against hers. "Merry Christmas, my ve." She grinned back. "Merry Christmas."

* * * * *

Dear Reader,

I had so much fun leading Ian and Gina on a merry chase. I hope you enjoyed the ride along with them. *A Silent Pursuit* is mostly about Ian's love of Gina and his steadfast approach to showing her what a great guy he is. And the fact that he kept her alive helped seal the deal for her. To me integrity and honor are so important. As Christians, we are called by God to live our lives based on a higher standard than what the world calls for. It's not easy and of course we fail, but thank goodness for forgiveness and unlimited chances! And thank goodness we don't have a God that requires perfection. But that doesn't mean we shouldn't strive for it, to constantly be reaching for that goal of being like Christ, perfect in every way. Again, thanks for joining Gina and Ian on their pursuit of justice and love. I hope you liked the ending as much as I did!

You can find me online at www.lynetteeason.com and love to hear from readers at lynetteeason@lynetteeason.com.

God Bless!

Lynette Eason

QUESTIONS FOR DISCUSSION

1. Gina realized she was in danger and needed help. She'd put off asking the one person she knew could help her until it was almost too late. If we put a spiritual significance on that, the question is: Have you ever put off asking God for help until it's almost too late?

2. Ian comes to the rescue. He drops everything to do his best for Gina, promising he won't leave her. How does God do this for us?

3. What was your favorite scene in the book? Why?

4. Gina wasn't happy that she had to call Ian for help. She didn't understand why Mario would want her to do this or why Mario trusted him. But she swallowed her pride and did it. And it changed her life. Have you ever had to swallow your pride and do something you knew was right but you sure didn't want to do it? What was the result?

5. Ian didn't want to believe Mario was guilty of something illegal or wrong. He continued to believe his friend was innocent, giving him the benefit of the doubt. Gina wasn't so sure. Which person would you have been had you been in the same situation? Do you give someone the benefit of the doubt, or do you immediately judge them guilty? How do you think God responds?

6. Who was your favorite character in the book?

7. Both Ian and Gina are believers and pray for God to keep them safe. How do you see God moving in the story? In their lives?

8. Who would you call if you were in trouble? Why?

9. What do you like about Ian's character? What do you think about his decision to leave the unit? Was that the right thing to do? Why or why not?

10. What do you think you'd do if you were in Gina's shoes? Would you blindly trust someone who a friend or loved one urged you to? Have you ever had to? Explain.

11. Do you think the title fits the story? Why or why not?

12. Ian and Gina didn't have a whole lot of time in which to fall in love, and yet they did. Of course Ian loved Gina long before she loved him. My parents met in April 1965, got engaged six weeks later and married on July 16, 1965. They're still together forty-four years later. What do you think about whirlwind romances?

13. Were you surprised by the bad guy? If not, what gave him away? If so, who did you think it was?

14. What do you think of Gina's decision to sell the farm? Did she do the right thing?

15. What do you think of Ian's method of proposing marriage? Did you like it?

Here's a sneak peek at "Merry Mayhem"
by Margaret Daley,
one of the two riveting suspense stories in the
new collection CHRISTMAS PERIL,
available in December 2009
from Love Inspired Suspense.

"Run. Disappear… Don't trust anyone, especially the police."

Annie Coleman almost dropped the phone at her ex-boyfriend's words, but she couldn't. She had to keep it together for her daughter. Jayden played nearby, oblivious to the sheer terror Annie was feeling at hearing Bryan's gasped warning.

"Thought you could get away," a gruff voice she didn't recognize said between punches. "You haven't finished telling me what I need to know."

Annie panicked. What was going on? What was happening to Bryan on the other end? Confusion gripped her in a chokehold, her chest tightening with each inhalation.

"I don't want—" Bryan's rattling gasp punctuated the brief silence "—any money. Just let me go. I'll forget everything."

"I'm not worried about you telling a soul." The menace in the assailant's tone underscored his deadly intent. "All I need to know is exactly where you hid it. If you tell me now, it will be a lot less painful."

"I can't—" Agony laced each word.

"What's that? A phone?" the man screamed.

The sounds of a struggle then a gunshot blasted her eardrum. Curses roared through the connection.

Fear paralyzed Annie in the middle of her kitchen. Was Bryan shot? Dead?

The voice on the phone returned. "Who's this? Who are you?"

The assailant's voice so clear on the phone panicked her. She slammed it down onto its cradle as though that action could sever the memories from her mind. But nothing would. Had she heard her daughter's father being killed? What information did Bryan have? Did that man know her name? Question after question bombarded her from all sides, but inertia held her still.

The ringing of the phone jarred her out of her trance. Her gaze zoomed in on the lighted panel on the receiver and saw the call was from Bryan's cell. The assailant had her home telephone number. He could discover where she lived. He knew what she'd heard.

"Mommy, what's wrong?"

Looking up at Jayden, Annie schooled her features into what she hoped was a calm expression while her stomach reeled. "You know, I've been thinking, honey, we need to take a vacation. It's time for us to have an adventure. Let's see how fast you can pack." Although she tried to make it sound like a game, her voice quavered, and Annie curled her trembling hands until her fingernails dug into her palms.

At the door, her daughter paused, cocking her head. "When will we be coming back?"

The question hung in the air, and Annie wondered if they'd ever be able to come back at all.

* * * * *

*Follow Annie and Jayden as they flee to Christmas,
Oklahoma, and hide from a killer—with a little
help from a small-town police officer.*

*Look for CHRISTMAS PERIL
by Margaret Daley and Debby Giusti,
available December 2009
from Love Inspired Suspense.*

Love Inspired®
SUSPENSE

TITLES AVAILABLE NEXT MONTH

Available December 8, 2009

CHRISTMAS PERIL by Margaret Daley and Debby Giusti

Together in one collection come two suspenseful holiday stories. In "Merry Mayhem," police chief Caleb Jackson is suspicious when a single mother flees with her child to Christmas, Oklahoma, where danger soon follows them. In "Yule Die," a medical researcher discovers her patient is her long-lost brother—with a determined cop on his tail.

FIELD OF DANGER by Ramona Richards

Deep in a Tennessee cornfield, April Presley witnesses a grisly murder. Yet she can't identify the killer. Until the victim's son, sheriff's deputy Daniel Rivers, walks her through her memory—and into a whole new field of danger....

CLANDESTINE COVER-UP by Pamela Tracy

You're not wanted. The graffiti on her door tells Tamara Jacoby someone wants her out of town. Vince Frenci, the handsome contractor she hired to renovate the place, wants to protect her. But soon they discover that nothing is as it seems...not even the culprit behind the attacks.

YULETIDE PROTECTOR by Lisa Mondello

Working undercover at Christmastime, detective Kevin Gordon is "hired" to kill a man's ex-wife. Yet the dangerous thug eludes arrest and is free to stalk Daria Carlisle. Until Kevin makes it his job to be her yuletide protector.

LISCNMBPA1109